REFLECTED GLORY

When artist Clive Hexley, R.A. vanishes, Chief Inspector Calthorp of Scotland Yard is called upon to look into the disappearance, and his investigations lead him to question Hexley's ex-fiancée, Elsa Farraday. Elsa confesses that she has murdered the artist. The girl's peculiar manner puzzles Calthorp, and he hesitates to make an arrest, particularly as Hexley's body cannot be found. It is not until Calthorp calls in Dr. Adam Castle, the psychiatrist investigator, that the strange mystery of Elsa's behaviour and the artist's disappearance is solved.

JOHN RUSSELL FEARN

◆

REFLECTED GLORY

Complete and Unabridged

LINFORD
Leicester

First published in Great Britain

First Linford Edition
published 2005

British Library CIP Data

Fearn, John Russell, *1908 –1960*
    Reflected glory.—Large print ed.—
Linford mystery library
    1. Detective and mystery stories
    2. Large type books
    I. Title
    823.9'12 [F]

    ISBN 1–84617–112–1

Published by
F. A. Thorpe (Publishing)
Anstey, Leicestershire

Set by Words & Graphics Ltd.
Anstey, Leicestershire
Printed and bound in Great Britain by
T. J. International Ltd., Padstow, Cornwall

This book is printed on acid-free paper

1

For quite ten minutes Elsa Farraday had been aware of the young man's scrutiny and it was commencing to make her feel embarrassed.

She continued quietly with her lunch, meantime glancing around the crowded London café — yet every time her eyes were drawn to the young man three tables away. And every time his gaze was fixed on her in polite but searching interest.

By degrees Elsa began to feel annoyed. This was downright rude, even impudent. Being young and attractive-looking, Elsa Farraday was by no means averse to a second glance, but this was too much.

Frowning to herself she lowered her eyes to her lunch and, for a time, tried to picture the young man mentally. He too was worth a long scrutiny, she decided. He was handsome in a dark kind of way with rather untidy black hair, straight nose, and well-formed jaw and mouth.

Perhaps twenty-five, and impeccably dressed. Yes, he was certainly —

'I say, I hope you'll excuse me . . . '

'Huh?' Elsa looked up with a start. The young man was standing beside her table looking down at her with a seriously apologetic face.

'I hope you'll excuse me,' he repeated. 'It just occurred to me that you must be thinking I've no manners, considering the way I've been looking at you.'

Elsa had gray eyes, and upon occasion they could be very cold. They were now. With her well-shaped mouth rather taut she responded:

'I was just thinking that you were providing ample evidence of the fact that the age of chivalry is dead!'

'Yes; I suppose it did look that way.'

The young man hesitated as though he expected Elsa would invite him to be seated on the remaining chair at the table. She did not. She continued eating her lunch as though be did not exist.

'I'm most awfully sorry,' he said, after a pause.

'That is the least you can be,' Elsa

responded, with another direct look. 'I don't think I have ever been so thoroughly — er — summed-up in all my life! And I don't like it! What's the matter with me? Or do you find a young woman something of a curiosity?'

'In your case, something of a revelation.' Then as he saw a warm tide steal into the girl's pale cheeks the young man added hastily, 'I — I mean in the artistic sense. You see, I'm Clive Hexley.'

'Should I be impressed?' Elsa inquired coldly.

'Well, that depends. I'm an artist. R.A., to be precise. I hope you haven't got the idea wrong,' Clive Hexley continued urgently. 'I was studying you so intently because you have just the exact face, throat, and shoulders I'm looking for. For a model, I mean. See here,' he finished, and handed over his card.

Elsa read:

Clive Hexley, R.A.
Cardenworth Studios,
Dell Road, Chelsea,
London.

'I hope,' Clive Hexley added anxiously, 'that that somewhat explains my extraordinary conduct.'

Elsa's expression slowly changed and the severity gave way to a slight smile.

'Yes, I suppose it does,' she admitted. She clicked the card between her fingers for a moment and became pensive; then Clive Hexley found her gray eyes upon him again. 'So you think I have prospects as a model, do you? That is . . . quite a fascinating thought.'

'I'm glad you think so.'

'Tell me about it,' Elsa suggested, and motioned to the solitary chair.

The young man seated himself and contemplated her again with earnest blue eyes.

'Well, you see, Miss — er — ?'

'It's Farraday. Elsa Farraday.'

'Well, Miss Farraday, I've been hunting for the past three months for a young woman with the right features to portray the essential mysticism of a feminine face. The painting is to be called 'Woman, the Mystery,' and naturally for a subject like that I have to use features which have just the right suggestion of the enigmatic. I require too the exact turn of the head and line of the throat which from the attitude will — '

'Mr. Hexley, you are an artist,' Elsa interrupted, smiling. 'I am not — in that sense, at least. I can only grasp the essentials of your work, I'm afraid. What you mean is: I happen to be the right type of person with the right type of features for your subject?'

'There's not the slightest doubt of it. Mind you, I know all this must seem dreadfully informal — for me to suddenly descend on a young lady who is a complete stranger and tell her that she has exactly the right face for a painting. But that is how my work is. I descend on all kinds of people, from beggars to drug addicts, from servants to film stars.'

'And you are a Royal Academician . . .' Clive Hexley noticed that Elsa had a lazy, fascinating kind of smile that gave just a glimpse of perfect teeth.

'Yes; and I'm proud of it,' he answered. 'Of recent years I have been quite successful, making up for the years when

I was not.' He smiled reflectively. ' 'Clive Hexley' on a painting — especially a portrait — actually means something at last. I even have several important commissions.'

'That's splendid,' Elsa said, somewhat absently, still apparently thinking of something else — and in the quiet moment that followed Clive Hexley had time to notice that she had night-black hair, perfectly contrasted by a rather absurd scarlet hat and scarlet stud earrings.

'You'll probably think I'm making the strides of a Gulliver,' he continued, 'but would you consent to sit for me? Everything will be perfectly all right,' he added, as she studied, him. 'Babs — or I should say Barbara — will be there too. That's Miss Vane, a very good friend of mine, and a professional model. She sort of takes care of the ethics when necessary.'

Ethics did not seem to be in Elsa's mind for she asked a question that had nothing to do with them.

'I suppose the subject of a painting in

6

the Academy becomes the focus for all eyes, Mr. Hexley? A sort of target?'

'Naturally the person in the painting is discussed,' he agreed. 'Why? Wouldn't you care for that?'

'I'd love it!' she declared, with surprising earnestness. 'In fact I can't think of a better way of attracting attention without being present in person.'

Clive felt that this was a most extraordinary statement, and he was still struggling to explain it to himself when the girl spoke again.

'My glory, such as it is, Mr. Hexley, is reflected. I said that I am not an artist in the same sense that you are. By that I mean I cannot paint or draw. I'm a writer.'

The young man's face lighted. 'A writer! Well, then, that surely gives us a kind of kinship, doesn't it? Writers, actors, and artists are all in the same class. I suppose I should know your works?' He looked somewhat ashamed. 'I'm afraid I read very little. Certainly I can't recall having seen the name of Elsa Farraday.'

'That's not surprising,' Elsa laughed. 'I use the name of 'Hardy Strong.' Quite successfully, too. My enjoyment comes from the fact that I achieve popularity, even fame of sorts, without having to do it with my personality. I'm just not the type to be on show. I'm — afraid of people.'

'I find that hard to credit — a girl as attractive and poised as you.'

'All you see is the outward shell, Mr. Hexley. There's quite a lot going on in my mind.'

Clive looked deeply into her gray eyes for a moment and then came back to his subject.

'About my painting . . . Do you think you'd care?'

'I'd be delighted. It so happens that I can spare the time just at present. I'm between novels, hunting round for ideas — and they don't come too easily sometimes.'

'Inspiration has no master,' he smiled.

'I know that, too . . . However, to become very commonplace for a moment: there is a fee of — '

'Which doesn't interest me in the least,' Elsa interrupted. 'Whatever it may be, donate it to a worthy charity. I'll pose for you because I want the extreme pleasure of seeing my portrait hanging in the Academy and having people discuss it — and me. You perhaps can't understand the thrill of being discussed and yet being just an onlooker at the same time?'

'No.' Clive looked at her frankly. 'I'm afraid I can't. It sounds quite an odd outlook to me. Matter of temperament, I suppose . . . Well now, what time would suit you? Beforehand, let me say that in summer I work mornings and evenings. From noon until six I wander around looking for material. That's why I'm in this café now — and this time my search has proven fruitful.'

'I'll be staying in London overnight,' Elsa said, thinking. 'I'm not returning to Midhampton — that's in Surrey — until tomorrow evening. I could sit for you to tomorrow morning.'

'That'll be fine, only . . . ' Clive looked troubled. 'I shan't be able to do it at one

9

sitting. You surely realize that? It will take several. Before we start how is that possibility going to fit in with your arrangements?'

'If you can make the sittings consecutive I can delay my return home for a week, or even longer — Or are you one of the temperamental geniuses who work in spasms at monthly intervals?'

He shook his dark head. 'My business is too serious to permit of temperament, Miss Farraday. I work as a man works at his office. Four consecutive mornings should do the trick.'

'Then it's settled then,' Elsa said, as he rose. 'I'll be at your studio at ten tomorrow morning.'

He reached down and shook the cool, slim hand she held up to him. For a moment he retained his grip on her fingers.

'I have my car outside, if there's anywhere I can drop you?'

'That's kind of you, Mr. Hexley — but I don't much care for cars. Even though I live out in the country I never use a car. In any case I've several calls

10

to make this afternoon. If any urgency should demand you get in touch with me I'm staying at the Claremont Hotel in Kingsway.'

'Right!' He released her hand, hesitating again. 'I suppose I couldn't pick you up tomorrow morning at your hotel? My place is a bit tricky to get at.'

'I'll find it,' Elsa assured him coolly. 'Thanks all the same. I'm a bit of an individualist in some things.'

He laughed. 'That's the creative instinct! Well, tomorrow morning, then . . . 'Bye for now.'

Elsa nodded and watched him hurry back to his table. He stayed only long enough to pick up the check, then taking his hat from the nearby pillar hook he headed towards the cash desk. Elsa saw him leave by the big glass doors and vanish in the busy main street.

'To think that there is a chance of the artistic world talking of Elsa Farraday,' she murmured. 'Perhaps it is just one real opportunity of having the world recognize me — in a way that could never obtain through my novels.'

She lighted a cigarette and pondered — until she realized that with the steady arrival of potential diners her table was needed.

2

When Clive Hexley had said that his studio was a 'bit tricky to get at' he had certainly not exaggerated. Elsa found it took her half an hour the following morning to trace it, walking in and out of the closely congested streets of Chelsea, most of them rendered all the more dingy by the merciless light of the summer sun; then at length she found Dell Road and stood considering it doubtfully.

It was narrow, cramped, and had all the appearance of a slum. She debated whether or not to forget the whole idea and recalled to mind a number of suspicions she had formed. For instance, Clive Hexley might not really *be* an artist: his card had only said he was, and that did not mean a thing. He might have some ulterior motive for his offer. Certainly, if he could work in a district like this he must have a mind superbly insulated from external impressions.

Yet even as she thought matters over, Elsa found herself walking slowly, studying the facades of the old-style buildings as she moved. There seemed to be a curious mixture of houses and business premises — then presently, on the other side of the road the sign CARDEN-WORTH STUDIOS caught her eye and she surveyed the building speculatively.

It was high, skylighted, and old-fashioned, every bit as unprepossessing as the rest of the buildings. Worn steps led up to a paint-blistered front door.

Elsa paused, musing, and staring at the place across the road — then as she was upon the point of walking away and forgetting all about the scheme Clive Hexley himself appeared at the top of the steps, the door swinging wide behind him. He was dressed in gray slacks and an open-necked shirt, the sleeves rolled to his elbows. Immediately he came hurrying across to her, a welcoming smile on his clear-featured face.

'I saw you from my studio window,' he explained, shaking hands. 'That scarlet hat of yours — I'd know it anywhere! You

14

ought to have let me bring you in the car, you know. This is no place for a nice girl to wander round.'

'You seem to find it quite satisfactory,' Elsa said, as he took her arm possessively and led her across the road.

'For business, yes — but then, I'm not an attractive young woman! At night it isn't a pleasant spot. I don't live here, you know: I've a flat near Regent Street.'

Elsa found that her suspicions of him had gone. Apparently he was a genuine artist after all — there were paint spots on his white shirt — and his personality was such that she found it hard to dislike him. He kept his hand on her arm as they went up the steps, then she preceded him into a short length of dreary, grimy hall.

'Top floor,' he said, and came close behind her as she ascended.

The top floor was five stories up, and here there were two doors, both of them open. One gave on to a small dressing room and storage space, a big mirror hanging on the wall where it caught the light; the other opened into a studio of surprising dimensions, its entire roof

15

composed of opaque glass through which the hot, diffused light of the morning sun was streaming. Elsa entered the studio slowly, interestedly, her last suspicions vanishing.

There were easels, chairs, stools, and a platform at one end with scenery propped against the wall near it. There were clean canvas frames, others partly finished, still others covered with cloths. A table had a few crocks upon it piled neatly at one end. An oil stove, extinguished, was in another corner. The floor was wooden, liberally bespattered with drops of vari-hued paints.

So much Elsa took in at a glance, then her eyes moved to the tall, blonde girl in a loose-fitting smock, idly smoking a cigarette, who came lounging towards her. She was definitely good-looking, and probably her figure also left nothing to be desired when divested of the formless covering she was wearing.

'This is Babs Vane,' Clive said, motioning. 'And here is Elsa Farraday, Babs, of whom I told you.'

'Glad to know you, Miss Farraday.'

Elsa's hand was gripped by long, firm fingers. 'Clive's been telling me all about you. In fact he's done little else since yesterday. Seems pretty sure he's found in you exactly the type he's looking for.'

Elsa only smiled. She was thinking at that moment that it would have been hard to find a more beautiful girl than Barbara Vane, with her natural golden hair, clear blue eyes, and straight features.

'I don't look mystical, you see,' Barbara Vane explained, as though she had read Elsa's thoughts. 'Blondes never do . . . '

'Excuse the untidiness of everything, Miss Farraday,' Clive broke in, pulling up a chair. 'Artists are notoriously Bohemian and I don't claim to be an exception. Let me have your coat, Miss Farraday.'

'And hat, surely?' she smiled, removing it and patting her night-black tresses.

Clive nodded and took the hat from her, then he took the light dust coat too. Barbara reached out a hand for them and took them into the adjoining dressing room through an open interconnecting doorway.

'How about some tea before we start?'

she enquired. 'I don't know about you, Miss Farraday, but I just can't exist without it.'

'Oh, I can survive — but as it happens I've had a long and thirsty walk this morning,' Elsa responded. 'I'll be glad of some, thanks.'

With a nod Barbara lighted the oil stove and placed a kettle upon it. Then she returned to stand near Elsa and rested her arm on the back of a chair.

'I can see what Clive means,' she said pensively. 'About the mystical look, that is. You've certainly got it.'

'Without doubt,' Clive Hexley agreed, turning to a bench and inspecting several tubes of color lying thereon. 'If I can just capture that look in the eyes, the turn of the head, and the general poise, I'll really have something.'

Barbara Vane seated herself, drew at her cigarette for a moment, then asked a question in her languid voice.

'I believe you write, Miss Farraday, under the name of Hardy Strong? So Clive was telling me.'

Elsa nodded. 'Yes, but I shan't feel

offended if you've never heard the name. I do fairly well, but I'm not a world-beater by any means — '

'Oh, but I *do* know your books. In fact I've read two of them, but . . . ' Barbara frowned and examined the end of her cigarette.

'But what?' Hexley asked, turning. 'It's the first time I've ever heard you mention Miss Farraday's work. You never said anything about it to me yesterday.'

'No, chiefly because I wanted to ask Miss Farraday herself. Do you really mean,' Barbara asked deliberately, 'that you — an obviously refined girl — write *that* awful stuff?'

'Awful?' It seemed a hard glint crept into Elsa's eyes.

'Not in the usual sense of 'awful' I don't mean. You write quite well — but the material is horrifying. In fact I should think you've started a new vogue in terror stories! I frankly admit, Miss Farraday, that after reading two of your books I got so nauseated I resolved never to read any more! I even pictured to myself what kind of a mind this Hardy Strong could have

19

to conjure up such elaborate ways of murdering people and disposing of them — Then out of a clear sky you have descended upon me! Not a big-fisted man but a retiring young woman. I just don't understand it.'

'I simply write what the public wants,' Elsa responded, with a shrug. 'And it pays. Certainly my work is in crime-horror thrillers, but that doesn't imply that I have the mind of an assassin, does it? As a matter of fact I only write at all as a sort of escape.'

'Escape?' Clive repeated, puzzled. 'From what?'

'Myself.'

At that moment the water in the kettle boiled and Barbara jumped up to attend to it. By the time she had prepared the tea and served it for the three of them the topic of Elsa's writing had slipped out of focus. They talked instead of Clive's work and everyday affairs, until Elsa was obviously at home enough to begin to pose for the portrait.

Under Clive's directions she took a seat by the window where the light fell diagonally across her face, and she found herself forced to gaze at the uninteresting view outside. From the tail of her eye she had a vision of Clive's right arm working at the canvas and, more remotely, Barbara moving about as she attended to odd jobs in the studio.

Elsa found that her first sitting occupied, in stages, about two hours, which brought the time close to noon — then Clive suddenly 'downed tools' and insisted on taking her out to lunch. It was a suggestion that seemed to give Barbara some cause for thought, though she did not make any comment.

'I know an ideal place — the Artists' Club — only a few streets away,' Clive insisted. 'Surely you can't refuse? Then I'll see you safely back to your hotel.'

Elsa did not refuse: she accepted the invitation quite willingly, though she could not help but notice the queer light in Barbara's blue eyes. It was an impression that remained with her so strongly she mentioned it over lunch.

'Oh, you don't have to worry about Babs,' Clive smiled. 'She isn't jealous, if that's what you mean. Matter of fact, she's no need to be. She's friendly with a young actor — Terry Draycott. You'll probably meet him soon. Come to think of it,' he reflected, 'this makes a triumvirate of the arts, doesn't it? Artist, actor, and writer.'

'Is he a well known actor?' Elsa asked.

'Well, he's a pretty celebrated supporting player, though he isn't in the star class as yet. Just working his way up. At the moment he has the villain's part in that new murder thriller at the Adelphi — 'Robert Had Two Knives.' '

Elsa nodded. She had seen the play advertised, but that was all.

'It isn't very long since we met,' Clive resumed presently. 'No more than twenty-four hours, yet we seem to be hitting it off all right, don't we?'

'Well, I suppose a certain amount of co-operation is essential between artist and model,' Elsa replied evasively. 'Just the same I do think, Mr. Hexley, that — '

'I wish you'd call me Clive.'

'Perhaps I will — later on. As I was saying, it's imperative that I leave London within the next few days. I have my own work to do, you know. You can finish that portrait of me in that time, surely?'

'It's debatable,' Hexley mused. 'I've hardly done anything yet — only sketched in the rough outlines. I may as well be frank and tell you that you are a disturbing influence. I can't concentrate on the painting because I'm concentrating on *you*. That never happens when I have Babs as a model. She registers blank negative on my emotions . . . Anybody ever tell you that you have aura — a queer sort of personal magnetism?'

'No. I don't believe I have, either. I'm one of the most retiring people imaginable.'

'Yet you write what Babs calls 'horrific' stuff. And she's a hard nut, believe me. Isn't frightened of anything as a rule. I think I'll grab myself a Hardy Strong novel and see what all the fuss is about.'

'I can't stop you doing that, of course,' Elsa said, 'but I'd much rather you didn't. You might get the wrong impression. I haven't really got a criminal mind, honestly.'

'I never thought for a moment that you had,' he said, looking at her in some wonder.

'I know, but after reading my work you might think otherwise. And I wouldn't like that — not now we've become friends.'

Clive smiled and almost unconsciously patted her hand as it lay on the table.

'All right, it's a promise. I won't look at your stuff. Not that I want to. I'd much sooner preserve the memory of the charming girl you are ... Tell me, whereabouts in Surrey do you live? You said Midhampton, didn't you?'

'Yes, but Midhampton's only a village, too small for mention on any map. I live in a small detached house called Tudor Cottage about a mile away from the village itself. I was born there, raised there, and when my parents died recently, within two months of each other, the place automatically became mine.' Elsa mused for a moment or two and then added slowly. 'They didn't leave me any money. What I have I've earned from my writing. But they *did* leave me something much more valuable than cash — freedom, and the opportunity to be somebody.'

'You mean they tried to prevent that when they were alive?' Clive asked interestedly.

Elsa nodded but she did not elaborate on the subject.

'The people in Midhampton have got to thinking of me as a kind of recluse — chiefly because I stay at home such a lot to do my writing and don't mix in the affairs of the village. Only on rare occasions do I visit London on business. And this time it seems to have developed into something more than just business, doesn't it? I've been given a chance to become famous through having my portrait in the Academy.'

'Well, there is that possibility,' Clive admitted, 'but don't put too much store on it. Critics are tough to please, sometimes. If my picture doesn't rate as high as it should nobody will care tuppence who the subject is . . . All in the luck of the game.'

'You must make it a masterpiece!' Elsa insisted, with an unusual earnestness.

'Promise me that you will? I so want to be known and talked about — And yet I also want to stay in the background and listen to the comments flying back and forth I — I get a sort of sense of omnipotence that way.'

'Which is pretty much what you said yesterday, and I still don't get the angle.' Clive gave a shrug. 'However, I'll put my best into the job, be sure of that. But promise me that you'll give me time to do the thing properly. One can hardly rush a masterpiece,' he added dryly.

Nor did he. In three more days, during which Elsa sat for him on three mornings and had three lunches, he still only had the rudiments of the painting in being. But the fact did not seem to worry him. To even be with her seemed to satisfy him — and though she would not admit it she found herself, when away from him, thinking almost constantly of his dark hair, amused blue eyes, and the clean-cut line of his jaw.

On the fourth morning Barbara Vane had a few comments to make, and she made them in the forthright fashion that

Elsa had come to know was characteristic of her.

'I begin to think that I've stopped around here long enough!' she declared.

The remark, coming into the midst of silence whilst Clive was painting, made him cease work and gaze at her in astonishment. Elsa too turned her head and noticed that Barbara was in her hat and coat instead of her normal smock.

'Since when did you become a stooge?' Clive asked, trying to sound patient.

'Apparently since Miss Farraday came! If you think I enjoy playing around here as a sort of chaperone — a job one usually associates with a middle-aged dowager — you're vastly mistaken! I'm sick of it, Clive! If you're so keen on ethics you'd better find a new way to make them operate. I've had enough.'

'But, Babs, this is absurd!' Clive protested. 'You've always hung around here when it's been necessary for me to have a girl as a model — '

'And I've always disliked it!' Barbara snapped. 'Hang it all, the position's ridiculous! Isn't it unethical enough that

I'm here alone for days on end, acting as your model — '

'Of course it isn't! You're a professional model. That's no more unethical than a doctor and his patient — And all that apart, we're good friends who understand each other. I just can't think why you want to let me down.'

Barbara moved forward a little, a gleam in her blue eyes.

'How can you be so intolerably stupid, Clive?' she demanded. 'Do you think I *like* seeing you taken away from me?'

Clive put down his brush and gave Elsa a glance as she rose from her chair. Barbara looked from one to the other of them.

'It sounds to me,' Clive told her curtly, 'as though you're deliberately trying to create trouble, Babs. What about Terry Draycott? He's the one you've really fallen for, and you know it.'

'Him!' The girl threw up her hands. 'Good heavens, is that what you think? Because he pays me a great deal of attention and takes me out sometimes? I never even give him a second thought when he isn't present. It's *you*, Clive, and always has been . . . Oh, I know it isn't customary to bare one's emotions in this fashion,' she went on petulantly, 'but I'm the type who speaks her mind. The thing that I've seen growing before my eyes these last few days has finally got too much for me. I can't stand any more of it.'

'What thing?' Clive asked ominously.

'Don't act the innocent! You know perfectly well you're in love with Miss Farraday — even if you do still call her by her surname! And she with you, or I don't know my own sex.'

There was silence for a moment, Elsa gently biting at her lower lip and looking at the angry girl pensively; then suddenly Clive banged his fist on the bench.

'All right I *am* in love with Elsa!' he declared loudly. 'And I'll go on being so, whether you like it or not! I still don't believe you ever had the slightest regard for me, beyond ordinary friendship, that is. I know I haven't for you.'

Barbara took a deep breath. 'But for this — this woman, how much I might have done,' she whispered. 'I could have made you see that we are indispensable to one another. As it is it's ruined — for good. I'm clearing out, Clive,' she finished curtly. 'And I'm never coming back.'

'But, Babs, you can't! You've an unfinished contract and there are some pictures which — '

The door slammed behind the girl and there was the sound of her footfalls receding down the stairs. Clive rubbed his chin slowly and then turned as he realized Elsa was beside him.

'Let her go,' she said quietly. 'If she has a nature as jealous as that you're well rid of her, don't you think?'

'Well, I suppose so, but it's a bit of a shock. I've known her for such a long time, and she's right about being indispensable, you know — '

'Nobody is indispensable, Clive. If it's a model you're after, then what about me?'

Elsa turned gently on her heel and, delectable though her youthful figure was, Clive hardly seemed to notice it. He frowned hard to himself.

'Funny thing,' he mused. 'I never even guessed that she felt that way about me.'

'I did,' Elsa said, coming to a halt in her gyrations. 'I saw it in her eyes: that was why I asked you about her. It just so happens that we are a better match, that's all. Can't alter Nature, can you?'

Clive looked at her steadily. 'A moment or two ago, when Babs was here, I referred to you as Elsa — and I'm going to go on doing it. Just the same as you've taken to calling me Clive. The formalities are finished with, aren't they?'

'Of course.' Elsa took his hand and gripped it gently. 'Clive, since you've openly admitted that you love me, I've nothing to gain by hiding my love for you, have I? I mean that,' she insisted. 'These last few days I've been falling more heavily every minute, but I held off until I saw how Barbara reacted. Now we know where we stand.'

'Yes, of course we do,' he breathed, kissing her impulsively. 'And if it comes to needing a model — '

'I'm ready and willing,' she smiled.

'You have only to teach me whatever tricks there are . . . Oh, the whole thing's so simple,' she went on. 'You a great artist, I a writer. That sort of combination can focus attention on me as nothing else could.'

'There you go again, talking in riddles,' he muttered.

'No.' She shook her head. 'You'll see what I mean as you understand me better.'

He studied her for a moment as though trying to analyze her, then he turned aside to pick up a duster for his paint-smeared hands.

'For this morning,' he said, 'work's finished. We're going out this very moment for an engagement ring.'

She nodded eagerly. 'And this afternoon I'll go back home and clear up my affairs there. Then I can come back to London permanently.'

'I'll come back to Midhampton with you . . . ' Clive put an arm about her shoulders.

'But — but, dearest, that would be a waste of time! There's really no need. I can clear everything up very quickly.

32

Besides, it might look rather bad, you and I — '

'Oh, be hanged to that! We'll be engaged officially by then. Anyway, what kind of a man do you think I am?' Clive asked in wonder, lowering his arm. 'Since we're on our way to being married it's my job to help you fix up whatever you want. No reason why I shouldn't, is there? There isn't anything *peculiar* about this Tudor cottage you live in, surely?'

Elsa gave a worried smile. 'No, of course not, only I really do think — '

'I'm coming,' he said, with quiet decision. 'We'll catch the train for Midhampton immediately after lunch.'

3

At four o'clock the rattling local train, which formed a connection from Guildford, had brought Elsa and Clive to the rural station of Midhampton with its profusions of summer flowers. Here Clive chartered the solitary horse-drawn cab and, since he clearly knew Elsa well, the driver had only to be told to take her home.

'Quaint place you live in, anyway,' Clive commented, looking out on to the sun-drenched and completely inactive village street.

'If you only knew how much I hate it!' Elsa clenched her fists in her lap. 'I've seen it for as long as I can remember. It is one of the earliest of my recollections. It holds nothing for me except unpleasant memories — of scolding, of being told not to do this and not to do that.'

Clive gave her a serious, half puzzled glance.

'You mean your parents were strict? That it?'

'That's it. They believed in the policy of a child being seen and not heard, but they carried it to excess, and being an only child I received the brunt of everything. I think,' Elsa finished moodily, 'I only started to live when they died. And twenty-five is a pretty late age to start living isn't it?

'Not if you do it properly,' Clive murmured, and patted her left hand on which was the clawed bulging diamond he had purchased for her in London prior to lunch.

Since she said nothing further he spent his time gazing out of the window again. The cab left the village presently and followed a solitary tree-lined road. On one side of it were meadows, golden with the summer light, stretching away to the distant blue line of the Hog's Back. On the other side there was a peculiar darkness in the grassless soil. It looked as though an evil hand had spread itself over the landscape and commanded that no green thing should grow.

'That's Barraclough's Swamp,' Elsa explained, noticing Clive's rather mystified expression. 'It extends for about five square miles, and unless you know it thoroughly — as I do — it's a death trap. There are two paths across it, one of them true — which I use sometimes myself as a short cut to my home — and the other false, which leads right into the mire. Get on that, and you never get out!'

'Charming thought,' Clive murmured, with a little shiver. 'And where's your place? Can we see it yet?'

'In a moment, when we've rounded the next bend.'

He looked ahead with interest and after a little while there came into view, well back from the road and completely isolated, a detached house in perfect replica of Tudor style, low-gabled, slanting-roofed in red tiles, with — he noticed as they came nearer — diamond-shaped window panes. It was evident, however, that the gardens needed attention. Cultivated flowers were foundering in a choking wilderness of weeds.

'I've no time to bother with gardening,'

Elsa said, seeing Clive's look. 'And I don't like a gardener prowling about the place when I'm all alone.'

The cab stopped and Clive sat looking at the house pensively. 'Nice place,' he said approvingly. 'Once it's tidied up.'

Elsa stirred as he opened the door for her. As he alighted beside her in the road he asked a question.

'Do you want the cab to wait for us, or what?'

'No, that won't be necessary. We can walk back to the village when we're ready. At the same time I'll call on the estate agent. He's a sort of jack-of-all-trades who'll handle everything.'

Clive nodded, paid off the driver, then followed the girl along the front path to a portico of rustic-faced stone. She removed a key from her big, chrome-topped handbag and opened the front door.

Clive walked behind her into a square, tastefully furnished hall and then into a lounge leading from it. There was nothing unique about the room. It was light and sunny, windows at each end looking on to the back and front gardens, and comfortably furnished.

'Sit down, Clive,' Elsa said. 'I'll fix up some tea and sandwiches for us — '

'But surely I can help you?'

'There's no need. Really.'

But since he was insistent, she said no more and he wandered after her into the kitchen. He stood against the doorway, watching her make preparations, unable to help her because he did not know where to find anything. Then he frowned a little as he caught sight of the big cupboard doors over the stove. They were firmly closed and secured with six shiny-headed screws down the sides.

'That's a queer idea, isn't it?' he asked, and Elsa glanced above her head.

'Oh, you mean the doors? That was my father's idea. They used to keep swinging out a lot and he was always banging his head on them. One day he got really mad and screwed them up.'

'And you've left them like that? They only want new catches. Think of the cupboard room you're losing.'

'I'm not bothered. One person doesn't

need a lot of cupboard room, anyway.'

Elsa completed the sandwiches and made tea without explaining matters any further. As she and Clive drank it in the lounge Clive glanced about him.

'Seems a pity to have to sell this place up,' he mused. 'So quiet and restful. I believe I really could paint masterpieces here. So much better than in that rather squalid studio of mine.'

'My only wish,' Elsa answered quietly, 'now I've got the opportunity is to get away from this place. I know every stick and stone of it. As I told you, I was born in it. I must get away from it, Clive. To settle down here to married life would be just too much for me.'

He smiled. 'Okay. We'll use my London flat until we can find something larger. Now, what things do you want to keep, and what to sell? You'd better make an inventory, then the estate agent will know what he's doing.'

Elsa nodded and reached out to the bureau near her elbow. Drawing a sheet of paper from it she began to jot down items as they occurred to her. Clive watched her for a moment, then with a sandwich half way to his mouth he paused, looking at a door in a corner of the room. He had noticed it when he had first entered the room, but at that time the angle of sunlight had cast it somewhat in shadow. Now it was perfectly clear, and the brilliant sunshine was playing on eight shiny-headed screws, similar to those in the kitchen cupboard, four driven home on each side.

'Great Scot, don't tell me that door swings too!' he exclaimed.

'Door?' Elsa looked at him, rousing herself from meditation; then she turned her head. 'That? There's a cellar beyond that. It used to be for coal, then my father had an outhouse made for it. In consequence that door, on the other side, drops down into a dangerous well — so it's sealed up. You may have noticed how the house juts on one side. That's the empty area behind that door.'

'Oh, I get it,' Clive acknowledged, resuming eating — but he rather wondered, deep down, if he really did. The passion Elsa Farraday's father seemed to have had for screwing up doors had had something of the quality of a mania.

'There, I think that's everything,' Elsa said finally, considering the list she had made and tapping her teeth with the pencil. 'Typewriter, manuscripts, blank paper, clothes and other necessities, of course — Yes, that's the lot.'

Clive looked at her and then glanced sideways at the list.

'There's far more on that sheet than just those items,' he remarked in surprise. 'What else is there?'

'Oh, just odds and ends.' For some reason she colored hotly and a defensive light glinted in her gray eyes. With a quiet possessiveness Clive ignored her obvious emotion and took the list from her.

'What's this?' he asked, frowning. 'The entire contents of the small room over the hall to be kept intact and stored until you give further instructions . . . '

'It's private,' she said, her mouth very firm.

'Okay, I don't want to pry, but it's hard to find flats these days and a whole extra room full of stuff is going to be a tough

41

proposition. What's in the room?'

'Oh, things. Personal.'

'Furniture, you mean?'

'Well, yes,' Elsa admitted.

Clive got to his feet. 'We'd better see,' he decided. 'I want to be knowing what I'm doing. Lead the way.'

She rose, shaking her head.

'I don't want you to see those things,' she said earnestly. 'In that room is something which is very dear to me. You'd just call it junk and probably laugh at me too. Please, Clive — don't ask me to explain. If it comes to it I'll find an extra room somewhere myself for them. I don't want it to be your responsibility.'

He hesitated, driven by the masculine urge to demand a better reaction from his wife-to-be; then his good nature settled the issue.

'All right, if you want to have secrets, have 'em! I wouldn't spoil your fun for worlds! Come to think of it, I have a secret too.'

'You have?' Her eyes were startled. 'What?'

'Oh, nothing very terrible,' he assured

her, laughing. 'Gosh, what a nervy girl you are sometimes! My secret is a slit in the bathroom wall of my flat into which I push my old razor blades. Ssssh! Don't tell a soul!'

'Oh, you — you idiot!' she exclaimed, laughing somewhat uncomfortably. 'I thought for a moment it was going to be something really important.'

'Like your mysterious furniture?' he asked dryly. 'And what are you going to do about your various things? Pity I didn't bring the car.'

'It doesn't signify,' she answered. 'Ted Husting, the estate agent, knows me well enough, and he's an auctioneer, real estate agent, remover, and heaven knows what else. I'll simply tell him what I want done and where to send everything, and that will be that. He'll find storage space for the stuff in — that room.'

'Uh-huh,' Clive agreed, and they were both silent for a moment.

Clive, indeed, was conscious of a grim impasse. Though he had tossed the matter off lightly his mind was still drifting in vague perplexity to whatever 'secret' the girl had.

'I take it that everything can go to your flat except the furniture?' she asked, picking up her handbag.

'Surely — Which reminds me, you haven't even seen it yet!' Clive gave a start. 'Hmm — we'll remedy that the moment we get back to the city. The address is Grant Apartments, 18a, Marton Street, West Central.'

'I'll remember,' Elsa said; then after a final glance about her she added, 'Well, that's all for now. Let's be going. Tomorrow I'll telephone my bank and have them transfer my account to the nearest London branch.'

Clive followed her out of the room and across the hall. She made sure the front door was securely locked and together they went down the pathway.

'I still like this district,' Clive said, giving his head a little admiring shake as he glanced about the hot countryside. 'All except the swamp, of course . . . Anybody ever get lost in it?'

'Plenty of people,' the girl answered quietly. 'Strangers as a rule who lost their way in the mist which settles at night around these low-lying parts. Far as I know about a dozen people have gone down at different times. Once, even, I heard one of them scream as he sank. It was in the winter — I never quite forgot it,' she finished, with a little shudder.

Clive glanced at her and gripped her arm reassuringly.

'This is daylight, and summertime,' he said gently. 'There's no earthly good can come of remembering those kind of happenings. Candidly, Elsa, I think you let your mind brood far too much on the unpleasant things of life. Maybe that's why your thrillers are so horrific.'

'No, that isn't the reason,' she answered, with a strange little smile. 'It's because — '

She stopped, glancing up, and Clive drew her to the side of the road as a two-seater open car came into view round the bend. The driver sounded the horn once and then applied the brakes. A dark, homely-looking young man with brown eyes, a soft hat pushed up on his forehead, contemplated the two seriously.

'Clem!' Elsa exclaimed, and for some reason there was a look of consternation on her face. 'Where on earth did you spring from?'

'Not a matter of springing. I was just coming along to take you out in the ordinary way. It's Thursday evening, remember — and that's my usual time for calling.'

'Thursday?' Elsa repeated vaguely. Then she seemed to remember. She glanced at her watch. It was ten minutes to six.

'At six o'clock on Thursdays I always call,' the young man said, a harshness in his deliberate voice. 'Why should this Thursday be any different?'

'I'd — forgotten,' Elsa said, making an effort to get herself in hand. She turned to Clive. 'This is Clem Hargraves, Clive, a very good friend of mine. This is Clive Hexley, Clem . . . '

'Also a very good friend of yours?' Clem Hargraves asked.

'As a matter of fact I am,' Clive responded, his jaw hardening. 'I can't say I altogether like your attitude towards my fiancée, either.'

'Your what?' Clem Hargraves gave a start, and Elsa gave an anxious glance from one man to the other.

'Fiancée,' Clive repeated deliberately.

'That,' Clem Hargraves said, 'definitely does it! Of all the cheap, low-down tricks! I'd never have thought it of you, Elsa . . . Oh, congratulations,' he added sourly, and raised his soft hat to a needless height. Then reversing the car swiftly he sped back up the lane and vanished in clouds of dust.

'Who *is* that character?' Clive demanded, as the girl stared helplessly after him.

'I was going to become engaged to him,' she responded, after a pause. 'Each Thursday evening he used to call for me in his car and we'd go out somewhere together — to Kingswood, or Guildford, to a show of some kind. Only with so many other things happening I'd completely forgotten all about him.'

'You had, eh?' Clive took her arm as they resumed walking. He had the feeling that there was something wrong here. Surely no girl could completely *forget* the man to whom she was all but engaged? It was more suggestive of her so timing things that they had been bound to meet him, which had given her the chance to snub him. Which seemed to throw a not altogether pleasant sidelight on Elsa's character.

'He's a commercial,' Elsa explained presently. 'Grocery, or something. I've known him for years, and since I've lived a pretty secluded sort of life he seemed to be about the only man near my own age with whom I came in contact. He used to call at the house when my parents were alive, for grocery orders. We became friends and . . . ' She raised a shoulder negatively. 'Well, I really had seriously considered becoming engaged to him. He'd asked me often enough. Then I met you and he went clean out of my mind.'

'Uh-huh,' Clive murmured, and he was perfectly willing to admit that the emotional impact *could* have banished all other thoughts from Elsa's mind.

'He's a dull chap,' Elsa sighed. 'Incredibly dull. He plods, whereas I like to trip. I don't think you can ever escape from yourself by just plodding, do you?'

'Having never tried to escape from myself — which seems to be a passion with you — I can't say,' Clive answered. Then he laughed slightly. 'Y'know, Elsa, come to think of it, we seem to have upset two people with our affairs. Babs Vane, and now this chap. Too bad, of course, but after all they shouldn't take so much for granted.'

They both became silent again, and it was a quietness in which they finished their journey to the village, Elsa leading the way along the high street to the estate agent's office. Across his window was a string of qualifications which in any modern town would have excited amusement — AUCTIONEER, REAL ESTATE, REMOVALS, PORTERING, DECORATING.

'Apparently the 'Admirable Crichton',' Clive commented, grinning.

Elsa smiled and seized the knob of the office's front door; then she frowned in annoyance, studying a card behind the glass. It stated briefly: AWAY ARRANGING FUNERAL. BACK FRIDAY.

'Which,' Clive sighed, 'seems to be that! Now what do you do? Leave him a note?'

'I can't do that; there are too many items. I'd be here all night writing them out . . . No,' Elsa decided, 'I'll telephone him from London tomorrow. That'll be good enough.' She glanced at her watch. 'And if we want to catch that six-forty train for Guildford with the London connection we'd better hurry. Come on — the station's half a mile up the street yet.'

4

That evening Elsa saw the flat in Marton Street and also realized from its smallness why it was necessary for Clive to start an immediate hunt for a larger one in readiness for when they were married. The remainder of the evening they spent in a night spot of Clive's own choosing, and towards midnight they parted — Elsa to her hotel and Clive to his flat.

At nine the following morning he called for her with his car and drove her out to his Chelsea studio. Having achieved his object of becoming engaged to her he seemed convinced that the distraction of her presence would no longer worry him in completing the portrait of her.

Another form of distraction was waiting outside the studio door, however, as the two discovered when they had mounted to the fifth floor.

'Hello, Clive,' Barbara Vane greeted, with a kind of sulky friendliness.

'Huh! The prodigal!' Clive ejaculated, gazing at her as he fumbled for his keys. 'What brought you back, anyway? I thought you'd gone out of my life forever.'

'Anybody is entitled to second thoughts,' Barbara answered, and glanced at Elsa. ''Morning, Elsa,' she added briefly.

Elsa did not reply. She just gazed, coldly.

Clive opened the door and the two women went into the wide, glass-roofed expanse ahead of him. As he tossed down his hat he studied them, feeling very much as though he were watching two tigresses sharpening their claws for battle.

'Just what is the reason for this about-face?' Elsa asked at length, removing her hat and coat. 'If you have the idea that your coming back will break things up between Clive and myself you're vastly mistaken. See for yourself . . . '

Barbara languidly contemplated the bulging diamond on Elsa's finger. Then she removed her coat and threw it over a chair back.

'I didn't expect anything else but a ring

after seeing the way Clive had fallen for you,' she said. 'And, in any case I don't care. That's all washed up . . . But I got to thinking. I'm not exactly reeking with money, even if Clive is — and, Clive, you did say something about my running out on my contract?'

'Yes,' he agreed bluntly. 'But if that's all that's worrying you I'll release you from it and pay you up to date.'

Barbara said quietly, 'You've half a dozen pictures unfinished with me as the model. What do you propose to do with them? Throw them on the ash-heap?'

'Elsa will take your place. We've already arranged that.'

The blonde girl considered Elsa with cynical attention. A flush came into Elsa's pale cheeks.

'What's the matter?' she demanded. 'I've as good a figure as you, haven't I?'

'I wasn't thinking of that: I was studying your features. You can't change those in the paintings you've done, Clive: only *I* will do, and you know it. And need I remind you that some of those paintings are commissioned? They're not just for you to throw about as you like.'

Clive lighted a cigarette and mused for a moment.

'Yes, that's true,' he confessed. 'Truth to tell, I've been so concentrated on this portrait of Elsa I'd overlooked all the other stuff.'

'Then start remembering it,' Barbara advised. 'I'm no business manager but at least I know how to keep you on the right track — and I hope your fiancée will manage half as well,' she added dryly. 'The completion of those pictures means a good deal of money for you — and to me it also means a good deal in prestige, beside the fee to which I'm entitled.'

'Prestige?' Clive repeated, puzzled.

Barbara spread her hands. 'I have to find another job as a model somewhere, don't I? When I apply for it I want to be able to point to these commissioned portraits with myself as the model. You owe me that much, Clive, even if only in the sense of a reference.'

'I think you've something more behind this,' Elsa said bluntly, 'and whatever it is I don't like it.'

'I think that whatever happens we'll never like each other very much,' Barbara commented, with a frank gaze.

'All right, all right, wait a minute,' Clive insisted, bothered by the vision of woman-trouble on his hands. 'Let *me* say the last word since I'm the artist concerned. As usual, Babs, you've got the right business slant on it. Very well, I'll complete the pictures in which you are posed, pay you up, and that finishes everything. Right?'

'Right,' Barbara agreed. 'I'll go and prepare.'

She turned and hurried into the adjoining dressing room. Elsa watched the door close and then swung back to Clive as he took off his coat and began to roll up his sleeves.

'What's the idea of giving her preference over me?' she asked angrily. 'We came here to finish my portrait — and instead you're swayed by a few lords on her part and forget all about me!'

'No, dear, it isn't that.' Clive patted her shoulder gently. 'You see, I happen to know Babs better than you do. If I were to spend my time trying to paint your portrait she'd stay here and keep on distracting my attention. She's definitely out to do it because she's piqued at my becoming engaged to you. If instead I finish off the pictures in which she is the model she has no excuse for staying — and out she goes. That's only logical, don't you think?'

'Well . . . ' Elsa pouted for a moment. 'I suppose so. I'd hoped we'd never see her again. All right, just as you say. I'll just sit around and wait and keep on the watch in case she tries anything.'

Clive gave a somewhat incredulous smile. 'What do you imagine she would be likely to try?'

'Anything! A jealous woman doesn't know any limits. She might even try and ruin that painting of me.'

'I could do another one even if she did.'

Elsa turned away and settled herself on the broad, fabric-covered top of the chesterfield under the main window. She lighted a cigarette and reclined, watching. After a while the superb, partly-draped figure of Barbara came into view again, and although she did not betray herself Elsa had to silently admit that her own smaller proportions would never have succeeded in duplicating the sweeping curves and graceful lines of Barbara.

Barbara gave one glance of her cynical blue eyes and then took up her position on the platform at the end of the studio.

' 'Water Nymph'?' Clive asked, searching through the canvasses.

'Might as well; it's the most advanced.'

Clive nodded, found the required canvas and perched it on the easel. He had hardly made three strokes with the brush, however, before there was a sharp rapping on the door.

'*Now* what?' he demanded irritably, and Barbara glanced round, drawing her draperies closer about her.

'Sounds like Terry,' she said. 'I know that triple knock.'

'Whoever you are, come in!' Clive called out, and then waited.

The door handle rattled and a shortish young man with very broad shoulders, dressed in gray, entered. He had dark hair, thickly brilliantined, a sawn-off nose, and an infectious grin.

'Terry,' Barbara commented. 'I thought as much.'

From the chesterfield Elsa considered him with languid interest as she smoked.

''lo, you two,' Terry greeted, grinning. 'Up to the old painting game again eh? Can't think what you see in it. Sooner do acting any time — Oh!' he broke off, catching sight of Elsa. 'I should have said 'you *three*,' he apologized. 'Sorry.'

'Miss Farraday, my fiancée,' Clive introduced. 'This is Terry Draycott, Elsa. Remember I mentioned him to you?'

Terry hurried over and shook Elsa's extended hand, then he gave a somewhat puzzled frown.

'Is there anything wrong in here?' he asked. 'Atmosphere seems sort of — chilly. Am I interrupting something?'

'Yes,' Clive told him frankly. 'I'm finishing a painting of Babs. To put it mildly, old man, either get out or dry up. I don't care which.'

Terry did not seem to hear. He stroked the end of his turned-up nose for a moment and then glanced from Clive to

Barbara — and back to Clive again.

'Wait a minute,' he exclaimed. 'I missed something. You said 'fiancée', didn't you? Miss Farraday?'

'Well?' Clive looked at him in silent challenge.

'I'm muddled,' Terry confessed. 'I thought Babs was the one you were going to — er — Wasn't it?' he asked bluntly.

'I never said so,' Clive replied. 'In fact I got the impression that *you* and Babs were 'that way' about each other.'

Terry shook his head, his frown changing to a scowl.

'Never. We're just good friends. Same interests, that's all. You jumped to conclusions, Clive.'

'So did Babs,' Clive sighed. 'Anyway, that's the way it is. Do you mind if I get on with my job?'

'Eh? Oh, no. Sure — sure.'

Barbara, however, stepped down from her pedestal on the platform, walked into the dressing room for a gown, then came back tying the gown sash about her waist.

'Am I permitted to ask what my model

thinks she's doing?' Clive asked bitterly, waiting.

'I can't sit there motionless whilst I'm waiting to know why Terry is here,' Barbara answered; and she looked at him questioningly. 'Something on your mind, Terry? That why you called?'

'Nothing more than usual. I simply dropped in to know how you'll be fixed for a date on Sunday afternoon. It's when we usually go out together, isn't it? I called at your rooms and they told me you'd probably be here.'

'I'll be free Sunday,' Barbara replied. 'And from the look of things I'll be free quite a deal once I've finished off what I have to do for Clive.'

Terry gave Clive a glance as he lounged near the easel, smoking. Elsa still remained silent, watching.

'To my way of thinking, Clive, you've handed Babs a pretty raw deal,' Terry said grimly. 'And me too, come to think of it. I've held off telling Babs how I really feel about her because I thought you were in earnest — and she thought you were too. I don't like to see a girl like Babs two-timed.'

'Oh, talk sense, you damned fool!' Clive snapped. 'How can you expect me to be responsible for the silly delusions you both had?'

Terry turned to Babs again. 'I'll make it up to you,' he said. 'And be mighty glad to as well. Sunday then, same time.'

She nodded; then when he had got as far as the door Terry paused and turned, feeling in the inside pocket of his jacket. To the surprise of Clive and Elsa he brought into view what appeared to be a beautifully carved dagger with a long, wicked blade.

'All right, don't get alarmed,' he said dryly, seeing Clive's look. 'It's only a trick dagger. Babs said she wanted to see it. I'm using it in the play I'm in.'

He went over to Barbara and showed it to her. Suddenly he stabbed at her and the hilt crosspiece apparently struck level with her breast and then the blade jumped out again.

'Mmm, very nice,' she laughed, taking it and studying it. 'Spring blade into the hilt, of course? I've heard about them and seen cheap ones, but never one as good as this. What do you think of it, Clive?'

'I'm not particularly interested,' he responded. 'All I know is that you're holding up my work. Why the sudden interest in that bit of theatrical property, anyway?'

'Oh, it just happens to fascinate me, that's all. I've seen the play and I just couldn't believe that such a beautifully made dagger could be phony. Now I'm satisfied.'

She poised it above her palm, drove the knife down, and the odd effect of the hilt on her palm and no blade visible through it made Clive smile a little. He held out his hand and took the knife from her.

'It is tricky at that,' he admitted. 'Take a look, Elsa.'

'What good would it do me?' she asked, without stirring.

Clive shrugged and drove the blade at his right hand — then he gave a sharp gasp of anguish, dropped the knife, and, cupped his palm in his left hand. Through his clenched fingers blood suddenly brimmed.

'What in — ?' Terry stared blankly as he picked the knife up. 'What happened?'

'The damned thing didn't work!' Clive retorted. 'It feels as though I've flayed my hand to the bone. You blasted idiot, bringing a fool thing like that in here — !'

He dashed across the studio and into the adjoining dressing room, Elsa fleeing after him. With his free hand he yanked some soft lengths of cloth out of a cupboard and bunched them into his palm, tying them in place.

'Clive, can't I help — ?'

He swung, his face white and taut. 'Only a doctor can do that. There's one down the road. I don't know what's happened but my hand just won't work. Won't even bend and it's bleeding like the devil . . . I'll be back,' he finished, and hurried out into the passageway.

Elsa hesitated over following him; then instead she turned back into the studio. She found Terry Draycott examining the knife blade minutely, working it up and down and cleaning it with a duster. Barbara was watching him. They both looked up as Elsa advanced slowly.

'How's he doing?' Barbara asked quickly. 'Was it a bad cut?'

'Bad enough to send him to the doctor,' Elsa answered, her voice stony. 'He says his hand won't work — the hand he paints with,' she added, her gray eyes glinting.

'I can't understand what happened,' Terry said worriedly. 'The blade works all right now — Look!' He flung the dagger downwards, but instead of it falling flat on the wooden floor the blade jammed again and the weapon swayed back and forth in the boards, transfixed by its point.

'It's stuck again!' Barbara ejaculated, startled. 'Say, that thing's dangerous. It doesn't work every time. The spring must be faulty, or something — '

'Get out!' Elsa breathed venomously. 'Both of you! Go on — *get out!*'

Terry stared at her, then at Barbara. Barbara gave a contemptuous smile.

'I'll go when I'm ready — '

'You'll go now,' Elsa interrupted, her voice harsh. 'What kind of a fool do you think I am? This meeting between you and Terry was deliberately arranged! I'm convinced of it. You had Terry bring that knife, fixed the blade somehow, and when Clive played around with it he damaged himself — So he can't paint! That's why! You arranged it deliberately to ruin him and to spite me!'

'Oh, don't be ridiculous!' Barbara retorted angrily. 'The whole thing was an accident. I didn't do anything to the blade — and Terry only brought the knife here because I asked him to. Just chance, the way it happened — '

'I don't believe it. Clear out, the pair of you!'

'If you think I'm going just because you order it you're crazy,' Barbara declared. 'I'm staying right here until Clive comes back and I hear how he is — '

Elsa turned to her big handbag on the table. She snapped it open and then swung round, a small automatic in her hand.

'You're leaving,' she stated. 'Now!'

Terry whipped the knife from the floor, wrapped it carefully in his handkerchief and put it back in his inside pocket. He said quietly,

'Well, I'm going anyway. I know which doctor Clive will have gone to. No use staying here, Babs — and that gun's unhealthy.'

Barbara's blue eyes gleamed angrily, but she was aware of the logic of Terry's words. Neither she nor Terry knew exactly what kind of a person Elsa was. She might, in her present mood of cold fury, fire the gun point blank.

'All right,' Barbara said curtly. 'I'll dress.'

'I'll see that you do,' Elsa snapped, and followed her into the adjoining room.

Barbara wasted no time. She bundled on her clothes, dragged on her coat, and left. Terry was waiting for her in the passage outside. Elsa moved to the door and watched them go down the stairs, then she wandered moodily back into the studio and returned the automatic to her handbag.

Wearily she went to the chesterfield and sank upon it. All the malevolent fury had died now from her expression and instead she seemed almost on the verge of tears. She looked at the half completed portrait of herself on the easel next to the painting of Barbara, then she sighed and shook her head to herself.

Half an hour passed before Clive returned. His face was grimmer than she had ever seen it, and deathly pale. His right hand had vanished now inside a pile of wadding and was supported in a sling.

'Clive — ' Elsa hurried over to him and caught his arm. 'What did the doctor say? How bad is it?'

He did not answer immediately. He sat down heavily on the chesterfield and passed his tongue over his lips.

'I feel groggy,' he muttered. 'There's some brandy over there in the cupboard — Pour me some out, will you?'

Elsa did so as quickly as she could, and under the influence of the spirit Clive seemed to recover somewhat.

'I — I saw Babs and Terry,' he said. 'They were waiting for me outside the doctor's — '

'Never mind them. What about you?'

'They said you ordered them out, with a gun.' Clive looked at the girl queerly.

'I'm glad you did,' he finished, his mouth shutting hard.

'They planned that business deliberately, Clive. I'm convinced of it.'

'So am I. Spite. Nothing else. I told them so, too. If I hadn't have cut myself so beautifully I think one or other of them would have 'accidentally' done it for me. Anything just as long as they ruined me.'

Elsa was silent for a moment, absorbing his words. 'Ruined you?' she repeated in a whisper. 'But . . . you'll get better, surely?'

'I've severed one of the main tendons of my hand,' he told her deliberately. 'My first and second fingers won't be any use for painting again. Good as paralyzed. In other words,' he added, speaking into a vast silence, 'an artist died this morning, Elsa. I'm washed up. Finished!'

'But — but your other hand?' Elsa cried. 'You can use that?'

'Don't see how I can,' he muttered. 'I've always worked with my right. I could never begin to do it with my left.'

A slow change came over Elsa's face, and it was an expression that Clive, studying her with his brows knitted, found impossible to analyze.

'What will you do then?' she asked, her voice brittle.

'I dunno. Anything except paint, I suppose.'

For perhaps half a minute Elsa remained motionless, her eyes fixed on him; then without speaking she suddenly wrenched the engagement ring from her finger and tossed it with a gentle clink on to the table.

'Elsa, what on earth — ?' Clive sprang to his feet.

She still said no word. Expressionless, she whipped up her hat and ducked before the wall mirror.

'Elsa, what's the idea?' Clive gripped her arm and swung her round, staring at her helplessly. 'You're surely not walking out on me?'

'What does it look like?' she asked bitterly. 'Where's the sense of keeping up the pretence? You could have given me fame; now it's gone. There's nothing else left, is there?'

'But dearest — '

'I'm glad,' she interrupted, 'that I

haven't yet 'phoned that estate agent to sell my place up. I'm going back home — where I should have stayed in the first place!'

She pulled free of Clive's grip, whipped up her handbag and coat, and left the studio. Dazed, he stood listening to her feet hurrying down the staircase.

5

Barbara Vane walked with Terry as far as her rooms in Dolphin Street, ten minutes' distance away. During the journey they had exchanged but few words. Events had happened so swiftly they had neither of them got things into proper focus. Finally it was the girl who spoke first.

'There's no doubt of one thing, Terry: he thinks the whole thing was deliberately arranged.'

'If he wants to think that, let him,' Terry growled. 'We know it wasn't so our consciences are clear.'

'Yes, but there's more to it than that,' Barbara insisted. 'In spite of all that's happened and the advent of that Elsa Farraday woman — whom I wouldn't trust across the street — ! I'm still deeply in love with Clive. I wouldn't hurt him or his work for the world. He's too fine an artist . . . So how do we start to convince him that the whole thing really was an accident? Heaven knows, he needs sympathy after what's happened. He may be mistaken, but judging from what he said he won't ever be able to paint again.'

'My suggestion, Babs, after the way he's thrown you on one side for Miss Farraday, is to leave him severely alone — particularly considering his readiness to think the worst of you.'

'From your point of view that's natural enough' Barbara sighed. 'But I know him too well. You can't get the man you love out of your thoughts that easily . . . Besides, I want to know if his hand is really as bad as he believes.'

'Which means?' Terry asked quietly.

'I'm going back to the studio, to try and explain matters.'

'And have that woman pull her automatic on you again? Incidentally, I wonder where she got it?'

'No idea, but it was there plain enough. Oh, if only I hadn't been interested enough in that trick knife to ask you to bring it!' Barbara exclaimed bitterly. 'The hopeless mess it's made of everything!'

'In a way I'm glad that you did,' Terry

responded, thinking. 'Otherwise the blade might have jammed whilst I was on the stage and I'd have been hauled up for manslaughter, or something. I'm going to report the dagger the moment I get to the theater. Anyway, Babs,' — and he patted the girl's arm gently — 'I think I know how you feel, and anytime you want me just let me know. You have a good idea how things are with me. I'd like you for my wife any day, 'specially now Clive's tied himself up otherwise. If you don't want that — okay. I'll still be your best friend.'

'Thanks,' the girl murmured, with a faint smile. 'You're a regular fellow, Terry.'

He nodded, raised his hat, and went on his way. Barbara glanced at the door of her rooming house, pondered for several moments, and then with a firming of her jaw retraced her way through Chelsea's drab streets to Clive's studio. She went up the stairs quietly so he would have no advance warning of her coming; but to her surprise both studio doors were firmly locked.

She knocked sharply on the main

73

studio door and waited, but there was no response. Disappointed, she turned away and wandered downstairs again, stood for a while at the main entrance door glancing up and down the dreary street. After perhaps ten minutes she glanced at her watch. It was 12-30. Knowing Clive's habits she was quite certain he would not return until evening.

So it was evening when she tried again — with the same result.

His absence, she realized, was explainable in a dozen different ways, but the part that troubled her was that, as time passed, it would become increasingly difficult to say the things she had planned. The longer she went without seeing him the harder it would be finally to convince him of the mistake he had made concerning her — and Terry.

The next day it also occurred to her that she had a legitimate reason for trying to see him: she was entitled to her fee for the sudden termination of her services. In the stress of events it had been the last thing of which she had thought. It was only when he had come to take stock of

74

her finances and considered the prospect of fresh employment that she recalled her uncompleted contract.

Again she went to the studio. It was still locked up; so she went to Clive's flat in Marton Street instead. But here again, to her dawning astonishment, the answer was the same. Going to the ground floor she sought out the proprietor of the flats.

'Mr. Hexley, miss?' he repeated in surprise. 'Why no, I haven't seen him for the last two or three days, come to think of it. Gone away maybe — or else I don't just happen to have noticed him.'

'But surely, if he'd gone away, he'd have left a forwarding address!' Barbara insisted. 'It isn't as though he's just — nobody. He's pretty important.'

'Yes; I realize that.' The proprietor shrugged. 'Sorry, but I'm afraid I can't help you.'

'Thanks anyway,' Barbara said, and feeling more baffled than ever she departed. In the street she pondered for a moment as to what she should do next — and her decision took her to the doctor who had dressed Clive's hand.

Being a busy man it was an hour before he managed to see her, and even then he was brusque when he realized she was not a patient.

'No, I haven't seen Mr. Hexley since he came here on Friday morning with his cut hand.' The doctor seemed to feel he had committed a breach of ethics in mentioning the injury for he asked sharply, 'Are you a friend of his, miss?'

'A very great friend, and I'm getting anxious about him. I can't find him anywhere.'

'Mmm, I see. Come to think of it he should have come in yesterday to have his hand re-dressed. That's a vital matter. You'd think he would at least attend to that for his health's sake.'

'Yes . . . you would,' Barbara mused, but she did not prolong the discussion since it would obviously have been useless.

From wonder her mood had changed now to alarm and it was the fact that Clive had not even bothered to have his injury dressed that troubled her most. That way he was simply asking for trouble.

Finally she came to another decision and put it into operation after she had had lunch. It was the last chance and it took her to Midhampton. Elsa's address she had jotted down — at Clive's request — on the off chance that she might need it some time.

Towards three in the afternoon, after the long walk down the lane, she reached Tudor Cottage, surveyed it, and then strolled up the front path and hammered boldly on the door. Though there was no response she did fancy that on two occasions she heard dim signs of movement within, and they seemed to come from somewhere above.

Frowning, she hammered again, as well as ringing the bell — but nothing stirred. Thoughtfully she looked about her. There was nobody within half a mile whom she could ask concerning Elsa's activities — but if there was nobody at home here she at least had the chance of making certain of the fact. So she went round to the back of the house and peered in at the windows.

Nowhere in the kitchen, back room

— which seemed to be a kind of study — or double-windowed lounge going straight through the house to the front, was there a sign of anybody. Yet she could have sworn she had heard slight sounds from an upper room, possibly the one situated over the hall, its window fronting the main pathway.

'Oh, forget it,' Barbara told herself briefly. 'They must have got married and gone on their honeymoon or something.'

But even as she said the words she had the instinctive feeling that they did not comprise the right answer. Clive was not the kind of man to marry in secret and steal away; and there had certainly been no newspaper announcements as far as Barbara had noticed. So, as she stood thinking, she presently drifted to bringing herself to a duty that she had known she should have performed much earlier.

She went to the police. The local inspector — beefy, burly, and by no means brilliant, sat rubbing a tufty eyebrow as she explained things to him in his cottage headquarters. Apparently, even if he had seen Elsa Farraday about

78

the district, he would hardly have known her.

'Well now, Miss Vane, don't you think you're making a mountain out of a molehill?' he asked presently, spreading his hands. 'After all, there isn't a scrap of proof that anything's gone wrong. The plain top and bottom answer is that Mr. Hexley and Miss Farraday have probably gone off somewhere together and they'll come back when they're good and ready.'

'Then what did I hear in Miss Farraday's house?' Barbara demanded. 'I heard something; I'll swear to it.'

'Probably a cat.'

'She hasn't got a cat — or a dog. She lives — or lived — entirely alone. She told Mr. Hexley as much in my presence. I can't quite explain it, inspector,' Barbara went on urgently, 'but I've got the most uneasy feeling that there's something terribly wrong somewhere. At any rate it can't do any harm for the police to look into things. As a private individual I can't do anything — but I will if you don't, and hang the consequences!'

'Well, we can't have you doing that,' the

inspector said gruffly, getting to his feet and reaching for his uniform-cap. 'All right, we'll go over to Tudor Cottage and see what we can find out — but there are limits to what I can do, remember. Regulations have to be observed.'

'Oh, blast regulations!' Barbara snorted. 'Get something done, for heavens' sake. For all we know Mr. Hexley, or Miss Farraday, may be dead!'

'Like as not havin' a fine honeymoon and not giving a thought to them they've left behind,' the inspector grinned. 'Anyway, my car's outside. I'll just run us over.'

He did so in five minutes and then sat at the wheel peering at the deserted Tudor-style home with its overgrown front garden. The place looked utterly deserted — and indeed something more than that. It had a definite not-lived-in aspect.

'Well?' Barbara questioned, her blue eyes reflecting her impatience. 'We can't accomplish anything by just looking, can we?'

'No — s'pose not.'

The inspector heaved himself out into the road, buttoned the top of his uniform jacket, and then in his best official manner opened the gate and walked behind Barbara's tall, slim form to the front door. He hammered violently and waited, breathing hard.

'You'll get nothing that way, inspector,' Barbara told him. 'I've tried it. Only thing is to break in.'

'That takes thinking about, miss. If I've no reason for doing it I — '

Barbara suddenly jabbed her elbow and it crashed through the stained glass in the upper half of the door. The pieces fell in silence on the mat in the hall.

'There you are, inspector: saved you the trouble. Now will you please get a move on?'

'Well, since you've precipitated things, I suppose I'd better.'

He reached his arm inside the break in the glass and felt for the milled knob of the Yale lock. He turned it back and opened the door. Barbara stepped ahead of him into the square, well furnished hall. She glanced about her.

'Hello there, anybody home?' she called.

Silence. The village inspector stood rubbing his massively heavy chin, as though he were uncertain what to do — which indeed he was.

'I have the feeling, Miss Vane, that I am exceeding my duty,' he said uneasily. 'If I'm getting mixed up with trespass — '

'Let's look around,' Barbara interrupted him, and she hurried into the lounge.

It looked exactly as she had seen it through the window, except for the fact that she now noticed the screwed door that Clive had seen. She went over to it and looked for the knob. It had been removed.

'Bit queer, that,' the local inspector commented, puzzled — and he left it at that before things became too involved.

'We'll see what else there is,' Barbara said, and hurried into the kitchen.

Here she and the inspector both gazed wonderingly at the vision of the screwed cupboard, but this time Barbara gave the problem scant attention. She continued on her way to the back room study. Here everything was normal — in so far that nothing was screwed up. Interested, she looked at the open writing bureau in which was a litter of quarto sheets, some covered with handwriting, others blank. She picked up the top sheet of a written manuscript and read:

She knew that there could be no escape from such daming evidence, but at lest even from this complte destruction of her life she could extract one profund consolation — as a murderess she could achive that which, as an innocent, she had nevr achieved.

'Somebody,' she mused, putting the sheet down again, 'doesn't seem to know how to spell properly.'

'This stuff doesn't tell us much anyway,' the inspector said unimaginatively. 'We'd better be having a look upstairs.'

Barbara nodded and followed him from the room and up the well-carpeted staircase. They looked in the two bedrooms and bathrooms and found them circumspect — and empty. Then they considered the closed door of what was presumably a much smaller bedroom occupying the area over the hall.

'Locked,' the inspector said, turning the knob and pushing gently with his shoulder.

'Well, we're not going away without knowing what's on the other side,' Barbara told him. 'Break it in. Go on — I'll take the responsibility.'

Barbara Vane had a way with her when she wanted things done, so the inspector hurled his beef into the panel. It cracked under the impact and a second blow enabled him to get his hand inside the door. He turned a key and swung the door wide — but he did not enter the room.

He, and Barbara too, remained motionless, completely unable for the moment to absorb the scene. It was not terrifying, ghoulish, or even suggestive of the sadistic. It was utterly bizarre and unexpected

Everything was in miniature — a doll's

room. There was a tiny, perfectly made table, a little bureau, quarter-sized beautifully carved chairs, a bookcase with bevelled glass fronts, the entire piece standing no more than two feet high. There were tiny books with microscopic titles, lacy-leafed shrubs in miniature stands — and amidst it all was a very big girl in very small surroundings. She was sideways to the doorway, seeming gigantic as she sat squeezed into a rocking chair, the top of which only reached above the small of her back. A huge pink bow flared on her black hair. She wore a pink, knee-length frock and white socks with black patent house shoes. In every way she was a vastly overgrown child, a feminine Gulliver in an incredible Lilliput.

She was staring at the smashed door in blank alarm, her mouth open in sheer horrified amazement.

The 'child' was Elsa Farraday.

6

Elsa got slowly to her feet and the inspector and Barbara still gazed at her in blank wonderment — Barbara more so than the official indeed for she remembered the poised young woman with the gray eyes, the pale face, and the automatic; but to the inspector Elsa's slightly built figure did not seem particularly incongruous in a child's clothes. Heavily developed beyond her age, perhaps, but nothing more.

'There seems to be some sort of mistake here,' he said, trying to get things into focus. 'I've broken in where I've no right and this youngster here is playing with her doll's house furniture — '

'This youngster, inspector, is Elsa Farraday,' Barbara snapped. 'And she's about twenty-five, at least!'

'Yes, I'm Elsa Farraday,' Elsa assented, vindictive fury in her voice. 'Why did you follow me here, Barbara? How did you get in here? I never heard you — until this door smashed open.'

'I broke in the glass on the front door,' Barbara answered, 'but since the pieces fell on the mat you probably didn't hear them.'

Barbara, now recovering from her shock, walked slowly into the room. As she gazed about her she felt like a giantess.

'What is all this confounded nonsense?' she demanded. 'You dressed up as you are and all this miniature furniture . . . Where is Clive?'

'What business is it of yours?' Elsa asked coldly. 'All I know is that you've broken into my home, into the privacy of my life, and I'm going to make you smart for it. And the law too! I'll report you for this, inspector!'

'All right,' he muttered. 'But it was Miss Vane's idea. She said she'd take the responsibility.'

'And I will,' Barbara said. 'Answer my question, Elsa — where is Clive? I've been trying to trace him since yesterday when he cut his hand, but he seems to have completely disappeared.'

'I don't know anything about him, and I don't want to! And I wish you'd get out!'

'Don't want to?' Barbara repeated, battling hard with the incongruity of the situation, for she found it difficult to realize that she was not talking to a child. 'You're engaged to him, are you not?'

'Not any more . . . ' Elsa sat down wearily on one of the tiny chairs and pushed a hand through her thick black hair. 'Please,' she implored, 'do leave me alone. I'm not doing anything wrong. I can behave as I like in my own home.'

'Just the same,' the Inspector said, clearing his throat, 'there is something about this which seems a bit irregular, Miss Farraday. I've all the particulars from Miss Vane. Apparently Mr. Hexley has disappeared, and the only likely explanation was that he had married you and you had gone away together on your honeymoon. Now even that possibility is disproved. Since you were apparently the last person to see him I'll have to ask you a few questions.'

Elsa got to her feet again and spoke sharply:

'I know enough about the law, inspector, to know that you are not really entitled to ask me anything. You've broken into my home without any conceivable reason and searched it. Where's your warrant?'

'Well, I — er — '

'You haven't got one!' Elsa snapped. 'Miss Vane here is responsible for everything; no doubt of that. And I'm within my rights in ordering you to leave. You haven't heard the last of this, inspector. I'll take the matter up with the Divisional-inspector for your area.'

The inspector seemed a trifle non-plussed by her ready grasp of the essentials of law and order, then he glanced at Barbara as she remarked:

'Elsa Farraday is a writer of crime thrillers, inspector — and for that reason I imagine she knows what she's talking about where the law is concerned. We'd better go. But don't think,' she added to Elsa, 'that the affair will end here. I mean to find out where Clive is.'

Elsa said nothing. She stood waiting as with a further rubbing of his heavy chin the inspector lumbered from the room and went down the staircase. Barbara hesitated in the doorway, studying Elsa in her astonishing child's get-up.

'For heavens' sake, Elsa, what *is* the idea?' she pleaded. 'At least explain that even if nothing else.'

'I've no reason to explain anything to you, Barbara, and I don't intend to. I'll answer questions to anybody who has the proper authority, but not otherwise. Now oblige me by leaving.'

Barbara went. Elsa waited until she heard the front door close, then she hurried into her bedroom and watched through the window as the inspector, Barbara beside him, drove his car swiftly away up the lane . . .

★　★　★

Barbara Vane, a woman of action, did not wait for Elsa to have the opportunity to lodge a complaint with the Divisional-inspector for the Surrey area. Knowing there was no telephone at Tudor Cottage, by means of which Elsa might speak first, Barbara insisted on driving to the Divisional-inspector's headquarters immediately. Nor did the local inspector raise any objections. The problem with which he was confronted was far too complex for his peace of mind.

Divisional-inspector Hayworth was a very different type from the local man — a square-shouldered, vaguely benevolent individual with a fresh-complexioned face. When Barbara and the local inspector had been shown into his office he listened in courteous silence to what they had to say, verifying each other as they went.

'I acted, sir, in what I considered were the best interests,' the local inspector concluded.

'I appreciate that, inspector, but you did exceed your authority,' the Divisional-inspector said, thinking. 'Miss Farraday was quite in her right in ordering you out — and if she goes further she can make things most uncomfortable for you . . . However, that can wait for the moment. It is the disappearance of Hexley which takes pride of place.'

'So I think!' Barbara declared, 'and I believe that Miss Farraday knows just where he is.'

'It's possible, of course,' the Divisional-inspector agreed, 'but before we have the right to question her we have to be sure where Mr. Hexley is *not*. In other words we have to know that he has, beyond a shadow of doubt, completely vanished without explanation. Not until we are convinced of that can we tackle Miss Farraday directly.'

Barbara looked worried. 'I've been everywhere that Mr. Hexley could have been, Inspector — and drawn a blank every time.'

'True; but the investigation must be much more thorough than that. It must also include a search of his studio and his flat, in case he might have met with serious mishap in one or the other and nobody is aware of the fact. Since Mr. Hexley lives — or lived — in the London area I'll hand that part of the business over to Scotland Yard. As regards Surrey

I'll make my own inquiries. As far as you are concerned Miss Vane, and you,' — the cold eyes settled on the local inspector '— you have done all you can.'

'To me,' the local inspector said, musing, 'it's suspicious in itself that Miss Farraday acts so strangely. Dressed up like a little girl amidst a lot of small furniture, when she should have been honeymooning with her husband — or something like it. What do you make of it, sir?'

'She might have been made up in readiness for a fancy dress ball; she might be a woman with delusions of childhood; she might be anything,' Hayworth responded. 'All that has to be sorted out. Leave the matter with me. I'll get some action quickly enough — and if I need you, Miss Vane, I'll get in touch with you right away.'

Thus dismissed, Barbara realized there was nothing more she could do. The Divisional-inspector saw her and the local inspector to the door and then returned to his desk. After thinking for a moment he raised the telephone and to the sergeant-in-charge in the next office he said:

'Get me the Yard . . . '

In five minutes' conversation he had made matters clear to Chief Inspector Calthorp of the Yard's C.I.D., and received his own instructions. Thereupon he left the office to begin his local investigations.

Altogether his inquiry occupied the best part of a week, carried out in a completely unobtrusive way. At the same time, in London, detectives working under Calthorp's orders, made their own inroads into the problem. It was a week and two days after Barbara Vane's visit to Midhampton before Calthorp and the Divisional-inspector met in the Surrey headquarters to exchange notes.

'Well, I've examined his flat and his studio myself, and not found anything,' Calthorp said, musing. 'Seems to be little doubt of it now, Hayworth — that chap Hexley has completely vanished. Not only that, there are quite a few people inquiring after him — the renter of his studio, for one, and a man who is expecting a commissioned painting for another. The proprietor of the London flat is wondering what he should do about letting it and disposing of Hexley's belongings if he doesn't return soon.'

'As I've mentioned, sir, in my reports,' the Divisional-inspector said, 'my local inquiries revealed that Clive Hexley was last seen in Midhampton here — at the railway station on the Friday afternoon. That was the day he cut his hand.'

Calthorp sat musing; he was a long-legged man, thin-nosed, partly-bald, with small eyes of an arctic gray shade.

'Which means,' Hayworth said at length, questioningly, 'that we must ask Miss Farraday a few things, sir?'

'Exactly. The sergeant — ' Calthorp glanced at Sergeant Dixon, his immovable henchman — 'and I will be going over to Tudor Cottage shortly for a word with the young lady. You did say in your report that you have the impression she may be a bit 'queer'?'

'Yes, sir; basing my conclusions on what I have discovered in the district concerning her. Apparently she was born in Tudor Cottage and has lived there all her life. Her parents died two years ago and after that she went on living a secluded life. I have definitely established that her age is about twenty-five — not ten or twelve as she looked on the day Miss Vane and the local inspector found her. She's also a writer of thrillers under the pseudonym of 'Hardy Strong' — pretty horrific things from all accounts. What few people she has spoken to in the village — mainly trades people — all say they were impressed by her apparent extraordinary desire to make herself famous.'

'I see,' Calthorp murmured, pondering. 'Hardly grounds for considering her 'queer,' Hayworth.'

'From all accounts, sir, that recent occasion was not the only time she's been dressed up like a child,' Hayworth added. 'I had a chat with two people, a man and a woman, who are local farmers around here. On different occasions last summer they each separately saw what they took to be a girl of ten or eleven seated in the back garden of Tudor House — which you can see from an angle of the road — and she was playing with dolls and a doll's pram. Of course it might have really been a child, even some relative of Miss Farraday's, but I can't discover that she has any relatives at all. So I'll gamble it was Miss Farraday, dressed up once again.'

'Hardly normal, but at the same time hardly crazy,' Calthorp reflected. 'We have to be careful how far we go, Hayworth. Since she is a writer it is even possible that she carries realism to extremes, and to study out her effects puts herself in character. Just a guess, but it's a thought. Best thing I can do is have a talk with her . . . Incidentally, I checked up on the automatic, which, according to Miss Vane, Miss Farraday has. Miss Farraday has a license for it, as a protection for herself in her lonely home.'

Calthorp got to his feet decisively and jerked his head to Sergeant Dixon. 'Come on, Dixon, let's see what we can get out of this young woman with the childlike notions . . .'

They went out together to their official

car and in his usual stolid silence Sergeant Dixon drove the seven-mile distance to Tudor Cottage. Drawing up outside the gate both men sat contemplating the quiet-looking house for a moment or two.

'Any ideas, sir?' Dixon asked at last. 'All sounds a mighty queer business to me.'

'No queerer than some problems we've tackled,' Calthorp told him. 'Carry on; let's see what we can do. If it becomes necessary I've a warrant entitling me to search. Depends on how co-operative Miss Farraday is.'

'Granting she's at home. If she's scented danger she's probably taken herself off.'

In this, however, Sergeant Dixon was mistaken. Elsa Farraday, pale but entirely composed, no longer dressed in the guise of a child, opened the door to them. Her gray eyes studied them questioningly.

'Good morning, Miss Farraday.' Calthorp raised his soft hat. 'I'm from the Yard — C.I.D. I'd like a word with you if convenient.' He displayed his warrant-card and added, 'This is Sergeant Dixon.'

'Come in,' Elsa said quietly, and held the door wider.

She closed it behind the two men and then motioned, into the lounge. They went in, glancing about them, seating themselves as she indicated chairs. She settled on the settee opposite them, still with that strange defensive light in her eyes.

'I've been expecting this to happen ever since that fool of a local inspector called upon me,' she said presently.

Calthorp cleared his throat. 'The local inspector was certainly indiscreet,' he confessed, 'and I am glad that you exercised tolerance, Miss Farraday, in not reporting him to the Divisional-inspector.'

'It's not so much a matter of being tolerant, inspector. I realized that I would probably not get anything out of it if I *did* report him . . . Anyway, that apart, what do you wish of me?'

'The answers to a few questions, which I'll make as brief as possible. Firstly, I think you should know that Mr. Hexley has, as far as our inquiries can establish, completely disappeared.'

'I'm afraid that is a matter which doesn't interest me.'

Calthorp frowned. 'But surely it should, Miss Farraday? You are — or were — engaged to him?'

'No.' Elsa shook her head. 'I broke it off . . . for private reasons.'

'When, and where?'

'Er — a week last Friday. It was at his studio in Chelsea — '

'You quarreled, perhaps?'

'I didn't say so,' Elsa retorted.

'True, but you would hardly break off the engagement otherwise.'

Checkmated, Elsa nodded slowly. 'Yes, we quarreled. Maybe it was mainly my fault. I did feel, though, that we could never make a success of marriage.'

'What was the nature of the quarrel?'

'Do I have to answer that?' Elsa asked quietly.

'No.' Calthorp shrugged and smiled. 'But I shall certainly find out the facts eventually. You can cut down time if you are willing.'

Elsa was silent, gazing meditatively at the carpet.

'Would it be about his inability to paint after him stabbing his hand?' Calthorp suggested, and the girl jerked up her head quickly.

'H-how on earth did you know about that — ? Oh, I see! Miss Vane told you, I suppose?'

'She told the local and Divisional-inspector, and they in turn told me. I checked up on it in London through interviews with Mr. Draycott and Miss Vane. I think it might save time to say that you broke your engagement because Mr. Hexley believed he would not be able to paint again.'

'Which you think was intolerably callous of me, I suppose?'

'I am not concerned with the emotional issues, Miss Farraday,' Calthorp answered, unmoved. 'Only in getting the facts. Am I right in my assumption?'

'Yes. I don't see what I have to gain by denying it.'

Calthorp studied her for a moment and

his eyes gazed beyond her to the room itself. For a second or two he considered the door with the shiny-headed screws down the sides but no change of expression came to his long, inscrutable face.

'Am I to understand, Miss Farraday, that you last saw Mr. Hexley at his studio a week on Friday when you broke the engagement?'

'That is so, yes. I haven't seen or heard from him since.'

'You are quite sure of that?' Calthorp insisted.

'Certainly I am! Why shouldn't I be?'

There was a pause. In a corner Sergeant Dixon was making swift short-hand notes.

Calthorp continued: 'We have the statement of the station-master at Midhampton that a youngish man, with his right arm in a sling, and answering Clive Hexley's description in every way, got off the London-connection train last Friday week about three-thirty in the afternoon. I cannot imagine whom else Mr. Hexley would have wished to see in this district except you.'

'It must have been somebody else,' Elsa replied, shrugging. 'Clive — that is, Mr. Hexley — is not the only man on Earth with his right arm in a sling. If on the other hand it was him, then he certainly did not come here . . . Why can't you believe what I say?' she asked impatiently.

'I have not said that I don't,' Calthorp answered.

Again the silence whilst Elsa contemplated him in grim suspicion; then she said:

'It surprises me, Mr. Calthorp, that you don't ask the most important question of all. You must be all burned up with curiosity about it — Why was I dressed up like a child in a room full of miniature furniture when Miss Vane and the inspector found me?'

'I am concerned, Miss Farraday, with the whereabouts of Mr. Hexley — not with the actions of your private life,' Calthorp responded. 'Unless you think that your — er — 'impersonation' might help to explain things in some way?'

'Not in the least. I dress like that when I wish to concentrate, and I go into that room with the small furniture to do it. There is nothing more significant in it than that. Some people bite a pencil, others dig gardens, still others go for long walks . . . I dress as I was at ten years of age because the mental condition thus produced enables me to think freely without undue responsibility.'

'Most interesting,' Calthorp said, without altering his tone in the slightest. 'Er — regarding the accident which Mr. Hexley had. Do you believe it *was* an accident — or intentional?'

'Intentional. I haven't the least doubt of it. I believe it was arranged by Miss Vane because she was bitterly resentful of the fact that I had, so to speak, taken Mr. Hexley away from her.'

'I see. And there is nothing more you can tell me, Miss Farraday?'

The girl thought for a while and then shook her head. Calthorp nodded and rose to his feet, smiling in his impersonal fashion. Sergeant Dixon snapped the elastic back on his notebook and thrust it in his pocket.

'Sorry I troubled you, Miss Farraday,'

the chief inspector apologized. 'All a matter of routine, you understand?'

'Of course.' Elsa rose, shook his extended hand, and saw him and the sergeant as far as the front door. When, they had gained their car Dixon waited for a moment, his eyes questioning.

'I take it, sir, that you didn't think it was worth while making a search of her place?'

'For what?' Calthorp asked quietly.

'Well, I — ' Dixon rubbed his ear. 'I don't exactly know. Might have been some sort of clue.'

'I don't think we'd have gained much, Dixon. No, I shall not indulge in any searching until I'm perfectly convinced that Miss Farraday has definite guilt attaching to her. At the moment we have nothing which can prove her story wrong, even though we can have our private suspicions about it.'

'I think she's a liar,' Dixon said bluntly.

'Maybe; but unfortunately we cannot act just on that assumption. What we are going to do is return to London and have further interviews with Mr. Draycott and Miss Vane — '

'But we've done that already!'

'Only sketchily, before we had the full details together with Miss Farraday's reactions. Doesn't it occur to you, sergeant, that if Hexley has been murdered, and his body mysteriously spirited away, there was a good deal of motive both on the part of Draycott and Miss Vane? More so, indeed, than on the part of Miss Farraday. We have only Miss Vane and Draycott's word for it that the knife incident was an accident. If, as Miss Farraday seems to think, it was deliberate, then it points to the real depths of jealousy to which Miss Vane, aided by Draycott, can sink. A woman who could do that would not hesitate at murdering the man who had been stolen from her.'

'Wouldn't she be more likely to murder the woman who had stolen him, sir?' Dixon hazarded.

'It's possible — but don't forget the old saying that 'hell hath no fury like a woman scorned.' It might well be that Miss Vane, realizing Hexley had deserted her for another woman, developed a sudden homicidal hatred of him — and perhaps killed him, with assistance from Draycott . . . Mind you,' Calthorp added, 'all this is pure theory, and I'm ready to have it exploded sky high. But it has to be taken into account before we really start to think of Miss Farraday as the culprit.'

'I suppose you think she was telling the truth about her little girl act?'

'I've no idea. It sounded logical enough. Frankly I don't consider it an important enough angle to worry about . . . Get moving, Dixon. Sooner we get back to London the better.'

7

Terry Draycott was in his dressing room, removing the make-up of the matinee from his features, when the chief inspector and Dixon entered, in response to his call to come in. He turned from the mirror with its horseshoe of lights and looked at them in surprise.

'Oh, it's you, inspector — How are you? Afternoon, sergeant.'

Both men nodded but ignored the chairs to which Terry motioned.

'This won't take long, Mr. Draycott,' Calthorp said. 'I'm just on a checking-up tour . . . In regard to that knife with which Mr. Hexley injured himself — you did say it was a trick knife and that by some mischance it jammed, didn't you?'

'That's right. I'm using a different one now. I reported the matter to the stage manager.'

'I understand. And where is the knife now?'

'I suppose he has it. I can ask him for you — '

'No, never mind. I'll see him as I go out . . . Tell me, Mr. Draycott, do you still insist that that incident with the knife was an accident?'

'Of course!'

'It seems to me,' Calthorp said slowly, 'that you could not have had a very great regard for Mr. Hexley — chiefly because he threw Miss Vane on one side for Miss Farraday. You, apparently, holding Miss Vane in high esteem, would not feel kindly towards Mr. Hexley on that account.'

'You're quite right, I didn't. I thought he played her a dirty trick, and I told him as much — but that doesn't alter the business with the knife. Please remember, inspector, that I had only brought the knife with me that morning. I didn't even remember it until I had been in the studio for a few minutes, nor did I know beforehand that Mr. Hexley had switched his attentions to Miss Farraday. You don't suggest that I suddenly decided to fake an accident, do you?'

'I'm not suggesting anything, but you could have known ahead of time from Miss Vane that Mr. Hexley had transferred his interest to Miss Farraday. Maybe even when she asked you to bring along the knife so she could examine it.'

'No.' Draycott shook his head. 'It was several days before when she asked me about the knife, before Mr. Hexley had met Miss Farraday. I didn't see Miss Vane in the interval, so of course I didn't know about him having left her in the cart for Miss Farraday.'

'Mmmm.' Calthorp picked up a jar of cosmetic, examined it absently, then put it down again. His cold gray eyes fastened on Terry Draycott's half made-up face. 'Mr. Draycott, at approximately three thirty in the afternoon of last Friday week, Mr. Hexley was seen at Midhampton railway station, after which he vanished. Can you give me an account of your movements from that time until now?'

'That's impossible,' Terry answered flatly. 'Just think how much time has elapsed!'

'I'm aware that my request may present difficulties, but in your professional capacity, Mr. Draycott, you should have a good idea of your movements. Most of your time must be taken up at the theater here. As for the rest of the time — Well, I'm asking you to fill in the blanks. I don't expect you to do it whilst I wait. When you've thought it all out let me have a detailed list at the Yard.'

'Which means I'm under suspicion or something?' Terry asked bitterly. 'Let me tell you, inspector, that I've never seen Hexley since he left the doctor's on the morning of his accident, after having had his hand dressed.'

'I am quite prepared to believe it, Mr. Draycott — but just let me have a statement of your movements, all the same . . . Now, where do I find the stage manager?'

'His office is on the right of the passage-way as you go out. The stage doorman will show you if you've any difficulty.'

'Right. Much obliged. Sorry to have bothered you, Mr. Draycott.'

Calthorp did not have any difficulty. His official status ensured that the faulty knife was immediately obtained and handed over to him. With it in a cellophane envelope he looked at the stage manager pensively.

'When was this knife handed to you by Mr. Draycott?' he asked.

'Er — ' The manager frowned and considered. 'It was a week last Friday — in the afternoon before the matinee. We tested the blade once or twice, and it jammed. So we discarded it.'

'And where has it been in the interval?'

'Lying in the property room. We've a big cupboard there where we keep a pile of effects like that.'

'I suppose anybody could have got to it in the meantime without much difficulty?'

'Quite easily,' the stage manager agreed. 'There's nothing in the property room which we consider worth locking up . . . I'd like to know,' he added, 'what all this implies?'

'To be candid,' Calthorp answered dryly, 'so would I! Many thanks for the knife, sir — and your co-operation. Come on, Dixon.'

Once more they returned to their car and then the sergeant asked a question.

'Why the knife, sir? We don't know that Hexley was stabbed. In fact we don't know a dam' thing about him. He may not even have been murdered!'

'Quite true,' Calthorp agreed, 'but at least we have one thing we can settle when we get back to the office — whether or not the affair that morning was an accident or not. The knife we've got should prove that. If it *does* jam, then we may safely assume that the whole thing was an accident.'

'Then, sir, why did you ask all those questions about anybody — meaning Draycott I suppose — being able to get at the knife without difficulty?'

'I'll explain that later. Drive back to the Yard, will you?'

'Not Miss Vane's place?'

'She can wait until later. I want to get this knife to work.' Dixon nodded and switched on the car's ignition. He drove swiftly back to the Yard through the busy traffic, then he and the chief inspector went up to their small, dingy office overlooking the Thames Embankment.

'Now,' Calthorp breathed, throwing up his hat on to the peg and then settling in his swivel-chair. 'Let's see what we can get out of this.'

He tugged the knife out of its envelope and examined it carefully.

'What about fingerprints?' Dixon asked, but the chief inspector shook his head.

'It'll be smothered in them. Nothing useful to be gained in that direction.'

'It's beautifully made,' Dixon said in admiration, and watched his superior drop the knife experimentally, point downwards, to the blotter. Each time the blade shafted back neatly into the ornate hilt.

'Seems all right,' Calthorp said, musing, and Dixon took it from him.

'Uh-huh.' The sergeant inspected the highly polished blade and the general design, then he held the knife above the wooden floor and dropped it down. It remained there, its point jammed into the boards.

'It — it stuck!' he ejaculated, startled — and the chief inspector sat staring at it fixedly.

Reaching out he yanked the knife free of the floor, then holding the blade in his handkerchief he began to work it up and down. Once or twice in the process it stuck, then freed itself.

'That settles it,' he declared, tossing the knife on the desk. 'It was an accident — which means that Draycott and Miss Vane have both spoken the truth. Even had they known beforehand of this dagger's dangerous tendency to jam, which I doubt, they could not have known *when it* would do so, could never have planned it so that it hurt Hexley in the way it did. Further, as I understand it Hexley took this knife and examined it of his own free will, striking at his palm with it. Nobody told him to, or even put the idea into his head.'

Calthorp became silent, considering the knife fixedly.

'So at one sweep we can discount Draycott and Miss Vane?' the sergeant asked.

'Well, I don't know about that — '

'But you just said — '

'I said we've proved that they spoke the truth about the accident, but that doesn't mean that between them — to pay Hexley out for deserting Miss Vane for Miss Farraday — they didn't 'take care' of him somehow. Only there is one rule which I have found infallible, Dixon — If people under suspicion are truthful in one instance they usually are in every instance, just as the lying witness always remains a liar. That being so I am inclined to think that when those two said they did not have anything to do with Mr. Hexley's disappearance they were again speaking the truth.'

'What, then, do you imagine Draycott might have done with this dagger?'

'It occurred to me that if he did happen to know a trick way of controlling the blade he might have adopted it to kill Hexley with. In other words, the *modus operandi* of a very clumsy murderer. He could have handed the knife in as faulty knowing that it would be consigned to the property room. He would have relied on the assumption that everybody would say the knife had been there all the time. Since nobody could prove otherwise it would have been quite a nice plan. But I guessed wrong. This knife is far too erratic to be used to kill anybody.'

'And we don't know that Hexley was stabbed,' the sergeant pointed out.

'Quite so. I based my theory on the belief that when found his body would have been found to have been stabbed. Now we have to look further ... ' Calthorp glanced at the clock. 'Have some tea sent in, will you? I'm more than ready for it.'

'Right, sir.'

Until the tea had arrived and the sergeant poured it out, Calthorp remained lost in thought, jotting down notes for his own satisfaction on the scratch-pad; then presently he tossed his pencil aside in annoyance.

'Y'know, Dixon, we're simply barking up a gum tree!' he declared. 'In fact we're presented with an almost impossible task. We don't even know if our man is dead — or, if he is, how he died. We don't know whether it was stabbing, strangling, shooting, or our old friend the blunt instrument. Mmmm — shooting,' he repeated, and chewed a sandwich slowly.

'Meaning Miss Farraday's automatic?' the sergeant questioned. 'You have the authority to make her turn it over if you want.'

'Yes — and an infernally long time after the possible event, in which period she has had ample opportunity to replace any missing bullets and clean the barrel. No, that's a blind alley . . . It is the missing body that has us bogged down. We can't even accuse anybody of murder without the body. Just hold an inquiry, think all the suspicious things we can — and move on. Case uncompleted. So says the law.'

There was a long silence before the sergeant spoke again. 'Since we have sort of eliminated Draycott and Miss Vane — at least for the moment — that leaves us either with Miss Farraday as the possible culprit, or some outsider whom we've not yet encountered. Or there is also the possibility that with the shock of his injury, added to by Miss Farraday's callous breaking-off of the engagement,

Hexley suffered a sudden attack of amnesia and is wandering around somewhere.'

The chief inspector shook his head.

'Amnesia isn't the answer, sergeant. The moment this business first reached my notice I had Hexley's full description and photograph — taken from a snap at his flat — circulated, which meant that police throughout the country would be on the watch for him. A man in his condition, with a badly hurt hand, could not have gone unnoticed by *everybody*. And his photograph appeared in the daily papers too . . . No, I'm quite convinced, more so than I have ever been about anything, that he is dead. And I'm pretty well sure that he has been murdered. It's just an instinctive feeling without proof, unfortunately.'

'Then in the absence of any other person with a motive, sir, we have to assume that Miss Farraday is the murderess. But how did she do it — and, even more puzzling, why?'

'I'll be hanged if I know why, even though it does seem pretty clear that she could not have held Hexley in anything like the regard she pretended when she broke the engagement the moment she knew that his power to paint had been destroyed. Presumably she saw the disappearance of the chance of marrying a famous man, to say nothing of the money that went with it . . . But whether her emotions were so upset as to make her wish to murder him is another matter. Doesn't seem logical somehow.'

'Assuming that she did wish to murder him,' the sergeant insisted, 'what do you think she perhaps did? Remember, she is a writer of thrillers and must have a pretty good idea of all kinds of ingenious dodges.'

'As I see it, Dixon, she could have done one of a number of things. We have more or less proved that Hexley was in her district before his disappearance. He could have gone to see her. She could have shot him, hit him over the head, or even perhaps have strangled him, though I doubt it considering her slender build. After that — Well, we just don't know. She perhaps disposed of the body somehow. Buried it — or even dismemberment and burning isn't out of the question in such a lonely spot.'

The sergeant chewed steadily for a moment or two, then he shook his head doubtfully.

'Somehow, sir, I can't picture that woman burning or dismembering a body. Besides, according to criminal annals, it's always the men who think of that gruesome angle . . . Suppose she perhaps shut the body up in a cupboard, or something? Until the hue and cry has died down?'

Calthorp started and nearly dropped his teacup.

'Great heavens!' he exclaimed. 'Of all the blundering fools!'

'Sorry, sir. Only a suggestion — '

'No, no, *I'm* the fool — not you! I've just remembered. Whilst I was talking to Miss Farraday I noticed a door in the lounge, secured down the sides with eight screws, four a side. They're new, I think — certainly shiny. You wouldn't notice them because your back was to that door whilst you were taking notes.'

'New screws?' the sergeant repeated quickly.

'So I believe . . .' Calthorp finished drinking his tea hurriedly. 'It's just possible we may have alighted on something, sergeant. We're going back to see Miss Farraday right away.'

8

Early this same evening Elsa Farraday had a visitor. At a ringing on the bell about six-thirty she opened the front door to behold a young man with a homely face and serious brown eyes standing in the porch. At the gate was a two-seater.

'Clem!' Elsa exclaimed, surprised. Then her expression changed. 'What do you want, anyway?'

'To talk to you.'

'Concerning what? Judging from what you said when you met Clive Hexley and me in the lane a week ago you never wanted to see me again.'

'Well — at that time that was how I felt,' Clem Hargraves admitted. 'But I've been having some serious conversation with myself since then, and I've also been seeing the newspapers. I have the feeling that you may be in something of a spot. With Clive Hexley having disappeared so mysteriously, I mean.'

'So?'

'So being your near-as-dammit fiancé before he came into the picture I decided I might at any rate still be your friend and try and help you out if I can.'

'Well . . . ' Elsa hesitated. 'I suppose I shouldn't ask you in — but there's nobody to see and I must talk to somebody. So — '

She stood aside and motioned. Clem entered the hall, tossed his hat on the hall stand, and then followed the girl into the lounge. Seating himself as she motioned to the settee he proffered his cigarette case.

'Now, start talking,' he suggested, when her cigarette was lighted. 'You know me well enough, Elsa: I'm a good listener. That is, talk if you can forget my bad temper that evening. Honestly, whatever may have happened between you and Hexley, I'm still in love with you, and I always shall be.'

'That's good hearing,' Elsa said slowly, her gray eyes deeply serious. 'I'm willing to admit, Clem, that I probably made a fool of myself and treated you most shamefully into the bargain.'

'Forget it,' he smiled. 'We all make mistakes. Anyway, what *has* happened to Clive Hexley? You of all people, engaged to him, surely ought to know?'

'I ought to, but I don't. And I'm not engaged to him any longer. You see, I broke it off — '

'You did?' Clem interrupted eagerly. 'Why? Did you find out that he wasn't any good?'

Elsa was silent. Clem's expression changed as he hunched forward.

'Well,' he said, 'whatever the reason, never mind. Just as long as you did break with him . . . What I've been trying to figure out is where you fit into the scheme of things. Have the police been making inquiries?'

'Only today. No accusations, no direct threats — no anything, but just the same I'm convinced that they think I had something to do with Clive's disappearance. Apparently the police think that because a man of Clive's description was seen at Midhampton station on the day I returned here from

London after breaking off my engagement with him.'

'And what are you going to do about it?'

'I don't know.' Elsa looked absently in front of her. 'But I'm pretty worried about it, as you can imagine.'

'Why should you be if you didn't have anything to do with it?'

'*If* I didn't?' she repeated, her eyes widening. 'Do you mean by that that you think — '

'Lord, no, of course not! Only a manner of speech . . . Look here, since that's the position, why on earth do you try and fight the situation all by yourself? You were quick enough about getting engaged to Hexley and, no doubt, had you gone through with the thing, would have been just as quick to marry him. Why can't you do the same as far as I'm concerned, then I'd be able to shoulder the responsibility as well?'

'I'm — I'm not so sure that I want that, Clem.'

He stared, at her. 'But why not? What's wrong with me? You've known me for years and we've often been together. Surely now it is more important than ever for me to share your troubles?'

'Yes, perhaps so, but . . . ' Elsa made a restless movement. 'For various reasons I don't feel now that I want to get married. I don't think you'd understand even if I tried to explain.'

'You can start to — '

A ringing at the front door bell stopped Clem Hargraves. Elsa looked up in surprise, glanced at the clock, and then rose. Going through the hall she went and opened the door. Clem got up slowly as she returned in advance of two men — one tall, in a lounge suit; the other in official police uniform with three stripes on his sleeve.

'Chief inspector Calthorp and Sergeant Dixon, Clem,' Elsa introduced, in a flat, hard voice. 'This is Mr. Hargraves, gentlemen, a very great friend of mine.'

'How are you, sir,' Calthorp acknowledged; then he glanced at the girl. 'I'd be glad if you could spare me a few moments, Miss Farraday. Private matter.'

'I'll go,' Clem said. 'See you some other time, Elsa.'

'Yes — all right,' she responded; hesitating, and with a nod to the two men Clem left the lounge, swept up his hat from the hall stand, and departed.

Through the window Calthorp's cold gray eyes watched him go down the front path.

'Well, gentlemen?' Elsa asked, seeming as though she were making an effort to compose herself. 'Won't you sit down?'

'I hardly think it necessary,' Calthorp responded. 'I expect to be moving about.' He produced a search-warrant from his pocket and handed it to her. 'My authority, Miss Farraday, for searching this house.'

Her cheeks reddened. 'What on earth for? What do you imagine I'm hiding?'

'I could hardly know, unless you care to tell me — but my inquiry has reached the point where a search of this house becomes necessary. Behind that screwed-up door, for instance — and also in that room with the miniature furniture.'

Elsa threw the search warrant on the table and gave a bitter smile.

'Very well, search,' she invited, shrugging. 'I don't think it will avail you much.'

Calthorp motioned his hand and Sergeant Dixon produced a short, strong screwdriver from his uniform pocket. Turning to the door he set to work on the eight screws, removing them one by one and putting them methodically on the seat of the chair beside him.

Elsa stood watching, tight little lines setting the corners of her well-shaped mouth. Calthorp's impersonal eyes contemplated her now and again; then he turned and gave the sergeant a hand to pull the door open, the screwdriver levering down the side.

It opened abruptly and Elsa turned away and looked out of the window onto the untidy back garden. Calthorp and Dixon found themselves gazing into a dark, dank-smelling space.

'Torch,' Calthorp instructed briefly, and producing a small one Dixon switched it on. The beam settled on a stone stairway leading downwards.

'Think we should?' Dixon murmured, with a glance at the girl's back. 'She might screw the door up on us!'

'Easily settled,' Calthorp said, and turned, raising his voice. 'Miss Farraday!'

'Yes?' she enquired, without looking at him.

'I'd like you to lead the way down here, please. This is your home and I wish to give you every chance to — '

'Go by yourselves!' she interrupted harshly, without turning.

Calthorp reflected, turned back to Dixon and said quietly, 'Okay, we'll risk it.'

The sergeant nodded and went down the steps warily, his torch beam waving. Calthorp glanced back as he followed, but there was no sign of Elsa in the doorway, its outline sharply clear in the streaming late evening sunlight.

The steps took a sharp leftward turn half way down and ended in a wide, utterly dark cellar that obviously went under the whole length of the house. On one wall was a rusty old door: on the other a grimed and cobwebbed wooden one, apparently belonging to a cupboard. On the floor lay a film of coal dust.

'A coal cellar, sir, at one time,' Dixon said. 'Long time ago too, judging from this iron door . . . ' He went over to it and flashed the torch beam on it. 'Rusted in, so there doesn't seem to be much use in looking for a body behind it.'

'Only lead outside to a grating or something,' Calthorp told him, and fingering the filthy knob of the wooden cupboard door he pulled it open and peered inside. There were two shelves, with some old object pushed in the back of the lower shelf. Certainly no sign of a body, even had there been room.

'Blank,' Calthorp said, sighing, and closed the door up again. 'All right, let's get back upstairs.'

They returned to the lounge and found Elsa still standing with her back to them, gazing outside. As Calthorp closed the door with a thump and motioned Dixon to replace the screws he asked a question.

'Why do you keep this door screwed up, Miss Farraday?'

She turned, strain still showing in the

lines of her mouth.

'Because it's dangerous. My father screwed it up and I left it that way to save the accident of opening it by mistake and falling down the steps into the cellar. It used to be the coal-hole, until an outhouse was built.'

'I see . . . ' Calthorp looked at the screws as the sergeant drove them home. 'How long since your father screwed it up, Miss Farraday?'

'Oh — two years, maybe. It was just before he died.'

'Mmmm . . . Well, now I would like to see that room with the miniature furniture — '

'*Why?*' Elsa demanded in surprising anger. 'What are you poking and prying about for? I know I can't stop you because you have the authority, but what are you looking for?'

'Since you force my hand, Miss Farraday, I'm looking for the body of Clive Hexley,' Calthorp told her coldly.

She stared at him, wide-eyed. 'What? Here? In this house?'

'If not his body, then some clue as to

132

his whereabouts, living or dead. Believe me, you'd help yourself and the police quite a lot if you'd drop this evasion of yours. We know that Mr. Hexley's disappearance is definitely connected with you in some way. It is for you to say whether we find out by the usual methods, at the cost of considerable nerve strain to yourself — or whether you prefer to explain matters in your own way.'

'If — if I were to give you the facts would you — leave that little room of mine unexamined?' Elsa asked, with an almost pitiful pleading.

Calthorp frowned. 'I can't guarantee that, Miss Farraday. It depends on what you have to say.'

'I have this to say . . . ' Elsa hesitated, biting her lip and looking at the chief inspector under her eyes. 'I — I killed Clive Hexley.'

A gleam came into Sergeant Dixon's eyes but Calthorp remained impassive. He nodded to a chair and the girl seated herself slowly. Settling opposite her he looked at her steadily.

'When?' he asked quietly. 'How? And

133

take your time, Miss Farraday. I want every fact . . . sergeant, take this down.'

'Yes, sir.'

'On the Friday I returned here from London, Clive — Mr. Hexley — followed me,' Elsa said, low-voiced, her fingers clenched in her lap. 'When you said you had information that he had been seen at Midhampton station you were quite correct. He walked from there to here. I got quite a surprise when I found him on the doorstep.'

'Then?'

'He wanted to come in. I told him I didn't want him to, that my association with him finished when I gave him back the ring. Instead of going away, however, he pushed into the hall, and then the lounge, and made himself thoroughly objectionable. I had to do something to defend myself so I made a grab at my handbag on the table. In it was my automatic, but I hadn't the time to get at it. So I did the only other thing I could: I hit Clive again and again across the head with my bag, the automatic inside making it pretty heavy. I landed one blow at the base of his skull, which, I suppose, must have been fatal. Anyway, he fell — Then when he didn't move and I examined him, I found his heart had stopped.'

'And what happened to his body?' Calthorp asked.

'When I found he was dead I became frightened,' Elsa said, breathing quickly. 'Then I remembered — you can only prove murder if you can find the body, so my instinct was to put the body where it could never *be* found. Perhaps it was a panic-reaction; I don't know. But I did spend all that Friday night dragging Clive's dead weight from here to Barra-clough's Swamp.'

'Where's that?' Calthorp asked shortly.

'Half a mile or so from here. It looks like ordinary land unless you're acquainted with the district. Actually it's deadly bog.'

'I might have guessed, had I known of that earlier,' Calthorp muttered. 'So you dragged him to the swamp and his body sank into it?'

Elsa nodded slowly, saying nothing.

Her gray eyes were filled with an abject horror

'I didn't mean to kill him, inspector!' she burst out. 'He behaved so abominably and I was so frightened I just struck, and struck, and struck.'

'I assume,' Calthorp said after a while, 'that you can show us where the body was thrown in?'

'Quite easily, but it won't do you any good, inspector. Nothing is ever recovered from Barraclough's Swamp. It swallows everything completely.'

'Just the same we'll investigate,' Calthorp said, rising. 'And I'd like to see that handbag you mentioned.'

'That? Oh, yes — ' Elsa got to her feet and went to a cupboard in the sideboard. She took out the bag and laid it almost gingerly on the table. Then she looked away sharply.

'I just don't like looking at it,' she explained, her eyes averted. 'It's just as it was after I'd struck him down with it, even to — to traces of blood on it.'

Calthorp looked at the bag pensively with its heavy chrome bar on the top, upon which were definite signs of brown smears. The bag was heavy, especially with the automatic in it. Carefully he unclipped it, tipped the contents on the table, then reclipped the bag and handed it to Dixon. He slipped it into a large cellophane wrapper.

'I shan't require these,' Calthorp said, motioning to the automatic, cosmetic case, and odds and ends. 'Just the bag for examination, that's all.'

Elsa nodded slowly. There was look of dawning wonder in her eyes.

'I would like to know,' Calthorp continued, 'why you are so anxious that your — er — miniature room should not be disturbed?'

'It just happens to be sacred to me, that's all. It's sacred for reasons that you would never understand.'

'So sacred that, in the belief that confession would leave it untouched, you have admitted to killing Mr. Hexley?' Calthorp asked.

'Yes . . . since you put it that way.' Elsa clenched her hands. 'I've told you everything, inspector: there's nothing more to be said, is there — beyond my showing you where the body was put? I shall plead self-defense, for I swear that is what it was.'

'I'm afraid you are a little ahead of the situation, Miss Farraday,' Calthorp said. 'I'm not going to arrest you.'

'But — ' She stopped, her mouth a little open and her eyes wide. 'But you must, surely? I've confessed to the crime! What more do you want?'

'The body.' Calthorp looked at her pensively. 'If it is found in the swamp and the injuries coincide with the attack described by you, then I'll have no other course than to formally charge you with the murder of Clive Hexley. Until that time I can do nothing. As for your confession, it is not uncommon to receive admissions of guilt in a murder case. I should have thought that you, as a crime writer, would have known that.'

'Of course I know it, but this is different! I tell you I killed Clive Hexley, and I've no doubt that the forensic department will find enough proof on that bag to convince you of it . . . ' Elsa

138

shook her head bewilderedly. 'You mean, then, that until you recover Clive's body I'm free, even though I am his self-confessed killer?'

'That's exactly what I mean. I don't make the laws; I simply help in administering them . . . Now, if you will be good enough to show us where you dragged the body, and the spot at which you submerged it?'

Elsa inclined her head briefly and frowned to herself. From the hall she took her dustcoat and slipped into it; then returning to the lounge she unfastened the French windows and led the way into the untidy weed-covered back garden.

'There,' she said, pointing, as the two men accompanied her. 'You can see Barraclough's Swamp from here.'

They looked and Calthorp nodded. 'I shouldn't have known it had you not told me, Miss Farraday . . .'

Elsa led the way to the bottom of the garden and indicated a broken piece in the wooden palings.

'I dragged him through here,' she explained, 'and across this field. You can see the ruts left by his shoes.'

She indicated them and Calthorp saw that they trailed across the almost grassless stretch ahead of them and then vanished in the weeds of the back garden. Without commenting he followed the girl, the uneven ruts clearly visible all the time, together with high heel marks in the soft earth which were presumably her own — until at length the half mile had been covered and the ground had changed from normal soil and rank grass to a dark, sinister expanse.

'There are two paths through this swamp,' Elsa said. 'One true and the other false. Just here is the true one — so follow me. It's only a narrow track so watch yourselves.'

The gouge marks went through the midst of the dark, evil mass and then suddenly stopped. Here there was a churning of the muddy earth with high heel marks mainly predominant.

'I pushed him in — there,' Elsa said, and pointed to a spot perhaps three feet away from them. 'It looks like ordinary ground — but just watch this.'

She looked about her until she found a fair-sized stone. Tossing it lightly she, the chief inspector, and Dixon watched it come to rest on what appeared to be solid ground — then gradually it sank and vanished.

'Conclusive enough,' Calthorp agreed, nodding. 'Thanks, Miss Farraday. For the moment I think I've seen all I need to see around here. I'll have men over to dredge this part of the swamp at the earliest moment. In the meantime I must ask you to remain in the district.'

'The law is a strange mass of paradoxes, inspector,' Elsa sighed, shaking her head. 'Here am I, freely confessing to having murdered Clive and thrown his body in this swamp, and yet you do not arrest me. It would almost be a relief if you would. Keeping the secret to myself for so long has been a tremendous physical and mental strain.'

'To say nothing of obstructing the law,' Calthorp reminded her dryly. 'However, I'll go into the matter again, Miss Farraday, when the body has been recovered . . . Let's be on our way, sergeant.'

The two men accompanied the girl back as far as the house, took their leave of her, and then returned to their car. Dixon aimed a questioning eye as he settled at the wheel.

'The Yard,' Calthorp told him, and sat back in the bucket-seat to muse.

The journey was half completed before he roused himself to start speaking.

'What do you make of it, sergeant? Any ideas? I've got my own, of course, but they're not necessarily correct. I'd like to check them against yours.'

'Well, sir, I don't quite see why you can't arrest her on suspicion, without actually charging her with murder. You could have done that.'

'Yes, I could, had I wished to cling to the exact letter of the law. Only . . . Only,' Calthorp finished, running a finger over his mouth pensively, 'I find it confound-edly hard to believe that confession, Dixon.'

'You do? It seemed straightforward enough to me.'

'Maybe, but consider certain factors. That screwed-up door, for instance. She said that it had been done by her father — two years ago! How have the screws remained shiny for two years? They're ordinary steel and I think that in two years they'd have gone far duller than they are. The implication being that she put them in the door herself. Why, I don't know.'

'Queer, sir,' Dixon admitted. 'No doubt of it.'

'She also said that Hexley made himself objectionable and that to protect herself she hit at him with her handbag. I am inclined to question both those factors. Remember, Hexley had only one arm he could use, which would not have been much use if he really did struggle with Miss Farraday. Secondly, she says that she struck him several blows, one at the base of the skull, which killed him. Well now, in the course of my career I've come across many people who have had the base of the skull fractured, but invariably the blow had been wielded by a strong man using a heavy instrument. The skull-bone, next to the sternum, is about the hardest bone in the anatomy. I find it hard to believe that a slimly-built young woman like Miss Farraday could have struck with sufficient force to kill a young man like Hexley — who, except for his injury, was quite strong. Nor do I think the small-sized automatic would have added sufficient extra weight to the handbag.'

'Mmmm . . . ' Dixon murmured, thinking — and he switched on the headlights in the darkening twilight.

'Add that to her story of dragging Hexley to the swamp and there disposing of him,' Calthorp concluded. 'I'll grant that the lonely district in which she lives would prevent anybody being likely to see what she was up to — but do you think she could do it? Dragging a man's dead weight for over half a mile in sloppy ground would take a good deal of doing, and most certainly it would for a woman of Miss Farraday's build. She's not an amazon by any means.'

'Then what do you think *did* happen, sir? Those gouge marks from Hexley's shoes, for instance — '

'Oh, those could have been made deliberately, same as her own shoe marks. The trouble is this business just doesn't make sense,' Calthorp muttered. 'It's hard enough to get a confession out of a person when they *have* a crime on their conscience: for one to confess to it when all the external factors are against it is well nigh incredible. And for such a trivial, irrelevant reason, too — just because I was on the point of examining that room with the miniature furniture.'

'Do you think it might have revealed anything to help us?'

'I very much doubt it. I'm more inclined to think that that room is simply a private den of Miss Farraday's, something she cherishes so much that she resents strangers looking at it. In any case, the local inspector saw it and there was certainly no body.'

Dixon negotiated a corner and thought for a while as he drove steadily onwards.

'If she didn't murder Hexley, sir, who do you think did? And where is his body actually?'

'I'll have the swamp dragged and see if

it turns up,' the chief inspector answered. 'If it doesn't, then I'll have to investigate in other directions. If it does, then maybe the marks of injury on Hexley's body will give us some clue. In the meantime we'll get this handbag examined and see if it has anything to tell us.'

9

The following morning the chief inspector received two things at once, finding them on his desk at nine o'clock when he arrived at his office in Whitehall. One was a complete statement from Terry Draycott containing a list of his movements as far as he could recall them — and the other was a report from forensic on the handbag. Calthorp tackled this first, throwing up his hat on to the peg and then settling at his desk.

'Bloodstains on the bag are in Group AB,' he murmured. 'Mmmm — the rare group. That may be a help. Hair definitely male, black, and from the head. Small sized medulla. Regular cuticular margins. Hair lodging in parts of the bag clasp . . .'

'Begins to look as though Miss Farraday might have been telling the truth after all, sir,' Dixon commented.

'We can get nearer to proving it when

we have samples of Hexley's hair, either from his recovered body or from combings taken from his flat,' Calthorp replied. 'The blood-group will be more difficult to identify without his body, or at least something he may have used which has a bloodstain of his upon it.'

'Then what about his hand? Surely he must have used something at his studio to stop the blood flowing when he cut himself? It might still be there.'

'Yes, that's a good idea,' Calthorp admitted. 'I think we'll pay a call there later — and at his flat, and see what we can find. Now, let's see what Draycott has to say for himself.'

He read through the itemized list carefully. Certain notations were ticked, and could be verified by witnesses. Where this was not possible the items were left blank.

'Four occasions where he can't prove where he was,' Dixon pointed out. 'If things start narrowing down to him again those four periods aren't going to look too good for him. He could have done just anything in those times — including murdering Hexley and cleverly concealing his body.'

'Yes, he could have done,' Calthorp assented. 'We'll keep the fact in mind, anyway. At the moment we have more pressing problems.' He put the statement away in the file and then said, 'You take the necessary men with you, sergeant, and have that swamp dredged. You had also better see the district coroner. Since Hexley was last seen in the Surrey area that coroner will be the one to hold an inquiry. It won't get us anywhere, but the law has to be covered. I'll tackle Hexley's flat and studio. It'll probably take both of us best part of today to do our jobs so we'll meet here again tonight and exchange notes.'

'Right, sir.'

Neither of them, however, was looking particularly pleased when they met that evening for their conference. Calthorp had already returned — indeed had been back some time judging from the tea things on a tray beside him — and was making notes at his desk when Dixon came in. The sergeant hung up his uniform-cap and then turned his thumb downward significantly.

'Might as well try dredging the Sargasso for buried treasure, sir,' he said, sighing as he sat down. 'I've had a party of the best men on the job all day and we got precisely nothing. We covered an area of about half a square mile from that indicated by Miss Farraday. In fact she came out to watch us at work.'

'Did she have anything to say?' Calthorp asked quietly.

'Nothing significant, if that's what you mean. Of course, she could have told us the body was there whereas it may really be in some other part of the swamp. Candidly, sir, I don't think we're going to have the slightest luck in scooping that morass. It's next to impossible to touch bottom, and the lower we get the more we stick. If Hexley's body *is* in there I think it will stay there — for good.'

'And so hamstring us in bringing any charge against anybody,' Calthorp said, thinking. 'Did you see the coroner?'

'I did, and he'll hold a routine inquiry;

then whatever else happens will be up to us.'

The chief inspector nodded, then got up and went to a steel locker. From it he produced two hairs, both set in a base of Canada balsam. He put them on the desk and studied them thoughtfully.

'Forensic have been working on these since eleven this morning,' he said. 'Just brought them in — set. One is a hair from the handbag and the other is from Hexley's hairbrush, which I got from his flat. They are identical in every detail.'

Dixon rubbed the end of his nose pensively. 'Which doesn't help us in our problem very much, does it? Or, if it does, it points more than ever to Miss Farraday. How did hair from Hexley's head get in her handbag clasp unless she did as she said and hit him?'

'It could have been specially put there so that we'd find it,' Calthorp suggested. 'Yet somehow . . . oh, I don't know,' he sighed. 'I'm getting more stuck every minute, and I freely admit it between ourselves. It is Miss Farraday's willingness to confess to the crime that baffles me, because I'm inwardly sure that she did not commit it. I'd get on firmer ground if I could find some bloodstain comparisons, but in that direction I've done badly. There isn't a thing in the studio that has bloodstains on it. I can only think that Hexley jammed wadding into his palm, and kept it there until he got to the doctor — which fact the doctor has as good as verified for me. He, unfortunately, has no bloodstained material for examination either. Once he had dressed Hexley's wound he burned the rough and ready swabs in the ordinary way.'

'So we're no nearer? We can't prove that the bloodstains on the bag belong to him?'

'Apparently not. We know that they're AB, and their rarity would make it unusual for them to be duplicated — but on the other hand it *could* happen. If we could only once prove that he *had* an AB blood-group we'd be entitled to believe it is his blood on the handbag. As things are, we're stymied.'

Dixon got up and poured himself a cup

of tepid tea from the pot on the tray. He drank it slowly and pondered meanwhile. Calthorp returned the mounted hairs to the locker, lighted a cigarette and drew at it slowly as he returned to his desk.

'I had further words with Miss Vane this morning whilst I was about it,' he said. 'The more I see of that girl the more convinced I become that she didn't commit this murder. She's somehow too *loyal* to Hexley — or at least to his memory now that she assumes, as we do, that he's been killed somehow. Besides, practically all of her movements can be checked.'

'Several of Draycott's can't,' the sergeant remarked.

'I know that, but in none of the times mentioned — which are not provable — would Draycott have had the opportunity to go to Surrey, commit murder, dispose of the body, and, come back. His theatrical engagement just would not have permitted him. And Hexley was last seen in Surrey, don't forget, on the afternoon of the day he cut his hand. I don't think he came back to London, where Draycott might have disposed of him, because the station-master at Midhampton can't remember ever seeing Hexley above once. As for Hexley's car, it's still in the public garage where he kept it, so he didn't use that. Again it narrows down to something which happened to Hexley, in or near Midhampton.'

'The only possible conclusion, sir, is that Miss Farraday *did* kill him, though not perhaps quite in the way she said. Since her story is open to so many doubts she perhaps invented it so that it would seem to give her grounds for pleading self-defense. Had she given the real story it might have proven her an out and out murderess.'

'The point that puzzles me,' Calthorp confessed, 'is that, as a thriller-writer with a knowledge of police procedure, she should be so determined to admit her guilt and expect to be arrested. She must know that without the body being produced she just cannot be. I can't think how to link those two points up.'

'If you ask me, sir,' Dixon said, in some disgust, 'that Miss Farraday is a puzzle no matter how you look at her. Dressed up like a kid, playing with dolls, choosing the moment when her boy friend splits his hand to break off her engagement to him, confessing to murder when she'd no apparent need — I give up!' He frowned for a moment, then a thought seemed to strike him. 'Just a minute! Maybe we've missed something. What about that chap we found her with last evening? What was his name now — Hargraves?'

'Well, what about him?'

'I was just thinking — Miss Farraday did say he was a very great friend of hers. He must have been to be in the house with her like that. Perhaps she is engaged to him, or something.'

Calthorp waited for the sergeant to unravel himself.

'I mean sir,' Dixon went on, 'that a man as closely attached to Miss Farraday as Hargraves seems to be might have had a reason for wanting Hexley out of the way — maybe so that he could get her for himself. He lives in Midhampton, so if we've nothing else we have at least another suspect.'

'Uh-huh,' Calthorp admitted, reflecting.

'If perhaps Miss Farraday is in love with Hargraves,' Dixon insisted, 'which she apparently was *not* with Hexley — or she would not have smashed up the engagement as she did — she might be shouldering the blame for him, knowing that he is the murderer. She knows you can't do anything without the body, but to make sure you don't even suspect Hargraves she's taking the blame herself. Maybe a sort of — of protective instinct.'

'Yes, it has possibilities,' Calthorp assented, after considering for a while. 'Maybe we have been a trifle lax in regard to Hargraves. First thing in the morning we'll go over to Midhampton again, track him down, and see what he has to say for himself. Since I don't want to ask Miss Farraday for his address, and so give away our moves, you'd better find a directory for the Surrey area and see if it's listed.'

Dixon nodded and headed for the office door.

★　★　★

In possession of Clem Hargraves' address, Calthorp and Dixon arrived at it in their car at eleven the following morning — a quiet suburban house in one of the village's side roads. An elderly, meticulously clean lady opened the door to them.

'Mr. Hargraves at home?' Calthorp inquired after identifying himself.

She shook her head. 'I'm sorry. He's a commercial, you know, and leaves fairly early, so he — '

'Perhaps, then, you've some idea when he'll be back?'

'I expect him at lunch time. He said he wouldn't be going more than ten miles today.'

Calthorp nodded his thanks and raised his hat. 'We'll be back then,' he promised.

And he was, with Dixon beside him. This time they were successful in catching Hargraves. He came into the front room, apparently still masticating part of his midday meal.

'You want to see me, gentlemen?' he asked in surprise. Then as he saw the faces of his visitors, and Dixon's uniform,

157

he gave a start. 'Why, I met you the other evening at — '

'At Miss Farraday's, sir,' Calthorp acknowledged, rising, and for the sake of confirmation he displayed his warrant-card for a moment. 'If you can spare a moment I'd be grateful.'

'Yes, of course I can.' Hargraves closed the door. 'Though this is a bit of a shock,' he confessed. 'My landlady didn't say the police: she just said two men. Being discreet, I suppose.'

'Possibly,' Calthorp agreed. Then: 'I believe you are a good friend of Miss Farraday's?'

'I am indeed!'

'Would you say an — *intimate* friend?'

'Depends what you infer by 'intimate',' Clem Hargraves answered guardedly. 'I've known her for some years, if that's what you mean.'

'Yes.' Calthorp gave a slow nod. 'That *is* what I mean. About how many years, Mr. Hargraves?'

'Oh — three or four.'

'And after three or four years you are on terms intimate enough to be invited into her home, with only Miss Farraday herself present?'

Clem Hargraves face darkened a little. 'What the devil do you mean by that? Trying to make something out of it?'

'Not at all; I'm drawing natural conclusions.' Calthorp's cold gray eyes did not move. 'I'm suggesting, Mr. Hargraves, that your relationship with Miss Farraday comes pretty close to being that of fiancé.'

'Quite right,' Hargraves agreed, without hesitation. 'I've always been extremely fond of Miss Farraday. I was on the point of becoming engaged to her when she met Mr. Hexley and in a sudden emotional tailspin fell desperately in love with him — or so she said. Then she realized her mistake, discarded him, and now . . . Well, we're right back where we started. Very soon I hope to become engaged to her officially, once this business of Hexley is cleared up and her mind is at rest.'

'Am I to understand,' Calthorp asked, 'that you took her engagement to Mr. Hexley with good grace? The sort of faithful watchdog attitude, wanting only her happiness regardless of your own?'

'Anything but it!' Hargraves retorted. 'When I found that she had ditched me for Hexley I got mad — madder than I'd ever been in my life. After all, it was enough to make me! She never even hinted what she was up to, then one evening when I was on my way as usual to call for her in the car for our little Thursday evening jaunt into town, she was coming along the lane as large as life with Hexley beside her. To my face she told me that she had forgotten all about my calling, and Hexley said he was her fiancé. What would *you* have done?'

'I am more interested in what you did, sir,' Calthorp answered unemotionally.

'I called her a two-timer, let Hexley see what I thought about him, and then returned to my rooms here in a boiling temper. But in time my anger cooled off, and when I found out the sort of spot she seemed to have got herself into — with Hexley missing — I went to see her and patch up our differences. That was the evening you came.'

'I see. And now your differences are reconciled enough for you to contemplate engagement to her?'

'Well, yes — but she's holding off for some reason. She said she didn't feel like getting married just at present. The Hexley business hanging over her, I suppose.'

Calthorp studied the room absently for a moment, then: 'Was the occasion in the lane the only time you saw Mr. Hexley?'

'It was — and quite enough too!'

Calthorp said: 'Obviously the disappearance of Hexley must be puzzling you as much as it is the police. Have you any suggestions to offer? Any theories to explain what might have happened to him?'

'I can only think of one possibility — that he may have wandered into Barraclough's Swamp, like many before him, and lost his life because of it, nobody knowing what happened to him. Not much of a theory, I know, but it is at least possible.'

'Yes indeed. In fact *anything* is possible . . . I'm afraid I am going to seem a nuisance, Mr. Hargraves,' Calthorp continued, 'but I'm going to ask you to let me have a detailed statement of your movements from about three o'clock on Friday week last, the day Hexley was last seen alive, up to today, stating where you have witnesses to prove it. Think it out carefully and send it on to me at the Yard.'

'What in the world for?' Hargraves asked in amazement. 'It sounds as though I'm on your list of suspects!'

Calthorp gave his wintry smile. 'I'm afraid you are. But that is nothing to be alarmed about, surely? All people connected — or known to have been connected — with a missing or dead person become suspect whilst the investigation is proceeding. I'm sure you'll be able to satisfy me.'

'What reason do you think I'd have for wanting to kill Hexley, anyway?'

'Isn't that a trifle artless, sir, when you have just said that you let Hexley know what you thought about him? With your intended fiancée snatched from under your nose, so to speak, without you even being consulted, you could hardly have *liked* Mr. Hexley, I imagine! See how it is? So — just you fix up that itemized list and let me see it. Routine: it has to be done.'

Hargraves sighed, his homely face worried. 'All right, inspector, if that's the way you want it. Fortunately I can prove most of my actions. Take it from me, I didn't kill Hexley — nor do I really know what has happened to him. I can only guess.'

'Quite so . . . Tell me, has Miss Farraday made any suggestions as to what might have happened to Hexley?'

'She, too, seems inclined to think that the swamp is the only answer. She has the idea that Hexley might have been on his way to see her, and mistaking the swamp for a field made an attempt to cross it, thereby cutting some distance off his journey down the lane. He could easily have taken the wrong path through the swamp and gone down.' Hargraves meditated for a while and then added, 'The Council should do something about that swamp, you know. Notices are put up regularly, but they sink. So do all efforts at providing railings. Doesn't seem any way to warn anybody. If signs are put on the solid grass little boys simply pull them down. Since everybody in this district knows the swamp and its danger I suppose the Council doesn't bestir itself as much as it might.'

Calthorp nodded slowly and then gave his slow, indecisive smile once again.

'Thanks for the various suggestions, Mr. Hargraves — and don't forget that itemized list as soon as you can. I think that covers everything for the moment, and I'm sorry I disturbed you.'

'Quite okay. Wish I could have helped a bit more.'

The chief inspector and sergeant took their departure and in the car they glanced at each other in mutual inquiry.

'Think he had anything to do with it, sir?' Dixon questioned.

'Hanged if I know — but I've certainly nothing much to go on. He had motive, and no doubt opportunity; yet though I imagine he might be an impulsive young man he doesn't strike me as the type who would let impulse get so far out of hand

164

as to make him commit murder. Further, if he did commit the murder I hardly think he would have been so free in his admission that he didn't like Hexley . . . No, Dixon,' Calthorp sighed, 'we're not much nearer. Nor do I think we shall be even when we get his itemized statement.'

'Then we're back to Miss Farraday?'

'Yes . . . and from the purely investigative angle I think we have done all we can. It has got us nowhere within reach of the right answer, so I think there's only one thing for it. Have an expert sum up the business and see what he can make of it.'

Dixon looked surprised. 'I don't see how anybody could be more expert than yourself, sir.'

'I'm thinking of Dr. Castle,' Calthorp told him, musing. 'The more I see of this business the more I think that there is something odd about Miss Farraday which we, as laymen, can't get into focus. A man like Castle might manage it. He's accustomed to handling queer people and he's saved our faces on more occasions than I care to admit . . . Yes, that's the next best move,' the chief inspector decided. 'Castle's always on tap when the Yard wants him. We'll get back to London and I'll go and see if he'll interest himself. Get moving, Dixon: I might be able to catch him before he closes his chambers for the day.'

10

Doctor Adam Castle, the psychiatrist and neurologist, and a behind-the-scenes expert for Scotland Yard when occasion demanded, had his chambers in Harley Street, and Calthorp and Dixon reached them a little after four o'clock. They had half an hour to wait, then they were shown into Castle's private office — a warm, luxuriant room with polished mahogany furniture, the shades half drawn over the sun-soaked windows.

'Well, boys, glad to see you!' Castle greeted, heaving up from his swivel-chair and coming forward with lumbering tread. 'Nothing like a visit from Scotland Yard to brighten one's outlook.'

Adam Castle grinned at his own remark as he shook hands, but the faces of the two Yard men remained serious. Both of them were thinking that with the warm weather Castle looked larger than his usual six feet two inches and heavier than ever. With a cherubic smile on his pink, baby-like face he motioned them to chairs and then resumed his own seat.

The sunlight back of him made his silver-white hair assume a halo.

'Well, boys, been getting yourselves tangled up again?' he asked genially. 'Or is this a professional call?'

'It concerns the Clive Hexley case,' Calthorp answered. 'You have probably read of it.'

'Yes — but off-handedly. I don't study the details of a crime case unless I'm actively engaged on it. Clive Hexley, eh? That artist chap who's disappeared so mysteriously?'

'The same,' the chief inspector said. 'I'm working on it, along with Dixon here, but there are lots of things about it which, in my opinion, don't come into straight police work. So I thought I'd have a word with you ... I'm very much puzzled by the young woman in the case, Elsa Farraday — otherwise known as 'Hardy Strong', a writer of thrillers.'

'I'll help you if I can, naturally,' Castle assented, the corners of his chubby mouth upturned as though he were enjoying himself immensely. 'What are the facts?'

The chief inspector gave them to him in a matter-of-fact voice. Castle did not interrupt him. He jotted down notes on the scratchpad with his fleshy hand. When the recital of details was over he sat back in his chair and wheezed asthmatically.

'Quite a pretty little business, eh?' he asked, his blue eyes twinkling.

'From my point of view, a confoundedly puzzling one,' Calthorp answered morosely. 'I'm not sure who killed Hexley: I'm not even certain that he's dead, and I can't make head or tail of the woman I should suspect. That's a nice mess for a C.I. to be in, isn't it? Sooner or later the Assistant Commissioner is going to ask me what I'm playing at, which is why I want action . . . Well, doc, there it is. What do you make of it?'

'Well, it's certainly an interesting business,' Castle said, tugging out a long-stemmed pipe and inspecting the tiny bowl. 'As far as Draycott, Miss Vane, and Mr. Hargraves are concerned, it seems to me that their actions are perfectly normal, and their reactions too. Clive Hexley himself remains as something of a problem. As for Elsa Farraday . . . ' Castle became silent, staring into distance as he lighted the pipe. 'As for her,' he finished, 'I think you're up against a remarkably complex young woman.'

Calthorp looked somewhat relieved. 'I'm glad you say that. I'd felt it all along, which was why I decided to ask you. Her emotions, to me, seem to be all mixed up, as though she's part child, part woman, part loyal, part vicious . . . Damned queer thing!'

'There have been queerer things,' Castle assured him, entirely complacent. 'So she dresses up like a child and sits in a room filled with miniature furniture, does she?'

'Apparently so. I have the word of Miss Vane and the Midhampton police inspector on that — and, partly, Miss Farraday's own admission of the fact.'

'Hmmm — quite remarkable, but not unique. And she has been seen playing with dolls and a pram?'

'So I understand.'

'And the moment she realized that Clive Hexley would not be able to paint she renounced her engagement to him? Yes . . . ' Castle brooded. 'Yes, that seems to run true to type,' he confessed.

'What type?' Calthorp looked puzzled.

Castle did not answer. He made several more notes and then glanced across the desk.

'I can't say much until I've seen the young lady for myself,' he said. 'And it isn't going to be easy. If she is what I think she is she'll be on her guard the moment she knows I'm trying to probe. I've got to have her at her ease, completely unaware that I'm really a bogey-man.' He chuckled fleshily. 'Since she lives in that remote spot, coming to London only occasionally, it's most unlikely that she will recognize me if I arrive in Midhampton in the midst of a motor smash.'

'*Motor smash?*' the chief inspector exclaimed, startled.

'I'll try anything once to achieve my

object. Matter of fact, London's getting a bit too stifling in this weather. I could do with a few days in the country. The wife was saying only yesterday that I ought to take her and Brendy for a vacation. So maybe I will, and include business as well.'

'Should I know Brendy?' Calthorp asked, puzzled.

Castle motioned a podgy hand to a round-faced girl with fair hair pictured in a silver frame on his desk.

'My daughter,' he explained, proudly. 'You've never met her? Hmmm — I don't believe you have. Sixteen — and home for the summer vacation.' Castle lunged forward, resting his massive forearms on the desk and considering Calthorp with his bright blue eyes. 'Consider the set-up,' he said. 'My wife, daughter, and I are on a motor trip: we meet with an 'accident' outside Miss Farraday's home. I'll borrow a car of ancient vintage for the job. If Miss Farraday has any Christian streaks at all she'll give us a hand. Once in her domain it will take blasting to remove us until I have found out all I want. And I don't think she'll suspect anything for a moment. Brendy will take good care to keep her off guard ... Er — I'll be a lawyer on vacation,' Castle added, grinning. 'I can borrow the address of a big friend of mine, and I'll get some cards rush-printed. Being a lawyer will be the nearest I'll ever get to making a fortune, I expect.'

'Okay, it's up to you,' Calthorp said, in his usual impersonal fashion. 'As you say, I don't see how Miss Farraday can know you are a 'plant' — '

'Oh! Has she a car?'

'No.'

'Splendid. That may make things better for me.'

'What do I do in the meantime?' Calthorp asked. 'Lie low?'

'As low as possible. Don't do a thing. The more Miss Farraday thinks you've forgotten all about her, the better. The freer her mind will become and, I hope, the more she'll talk.'

Calthorp considered for a moment, then: 'I suppose the thing is entirely ethical? You entering Miss Farraday's home under false pretences?'

'There will be no false pretences,' Castle chuckled. 'The 'accident' will be genuine — apparently — and if Miss Farraday wants to help why should we stop her? We're not *forcing* her to do anything: I'm simply using psychological reaction and guessing ahead what she'll do — Dammit, man, you Scotland Yard chaps use your wives, sisters, and daughters shamelessly when you want a woman angle to solve a case. Where's the difference? To preserve law and order any trick is permissible. I know just how far I can go, don't worry.'

Satisfied, Calthorp got to his feet with Dixon beside him.

'Okay then, doc, I leave it to you — and you'll let me know the moment you've got anything worth while?'

'Surely. But don't tie me down as to how long that may take. Miss Farraday isn't going to be such an easy problem to solve as you perhaps imagine.'

★ ★ ★

Towards half past three the following afternoon, when she had returned from Guildford to attend the adjourned inquiry on Clive Hexley's disappearance, Elsa found her thoughts interrupted by the ringing of the front door bell as she sat in her study writing. For a moment or two she sat puzzling, then it came again even more urgently. She put down her pen and rose.

In the porch way she beheld a round-faced, fair-headed girl without a hat, obviously distraught, dust smothering her neat gray two-piece and in smudges across her left cheek.

'Thank heaven there's somebody here!' she exclaimed in relief. 'I was beginning to think — There's been an accident,' she hurried on, gulping. 'In the car — my father and mother. I just don't know what to do. I think they're — '

'Where's the accident happened?' Elsa interrupted, impressed by the girl's panic-stricken youth.

Brenda Castle waved an arm behind her. 'Just outside your front gate — or rather a few yards down the road. Please,

175

would you help me? I'm all in pieces — '

'Of course I will.'

Elsa left the house quickly as the girl turned and followed her down the front path. Almost immediately, to the right, Elsa saw an ancient touring car with its engine telescoped into a telegraph pole. A big, heavy man with silver hair was slowly climbing out of the wreck, fingering his forehead painfully — though it was apparently unmarked.

In the front seat, next the steering wheel, a woman of middle age lay motionless with her head on the back cushions. The glass of the windscreen had been smashed in half a dozen places.

'Dad, you're all right then!' the girl cried, rushing towards him in relief and catching his arm. 'Oh, thank heaven — But what about mum?'

'I — I don't know, my dear,' Dr. Castle muttered, dazed. 'As a matter of fact I haven't yet realized what's happened.'

He appeared to make a tremendous effort to gather his wits, gave Elsa a bemused glance, and then with his daughter's help set to work to raise his 'unconscious' wife free of the car. They laid her down gently beside the wreck and Castle chafed her wrists and hands vigorously.

'You can't attend to her properly out here,' Elsa said, having summed things up. 'Come into the house where she can lie down. I'll give you a hand.'

Castle looked at her gratefully. 'You're most kind, miss — And maybe it would be best . . . To whom am I indebted?'

'I'm Miss Farraday — and that is my home back there. Your daughter came and told me about the accident.'

'Oh? She did? Good girl!' Castle rubbed his forehead again. 'You must forgive me, Miss Farraday. I haven't properly collected my senses yet — Now, Brendy, give me a hand with your mother.'

Elsa lent a willing hand too and between them the white-faced, middle-aged lady with the aqualine features and graying hair was transported from the dusty road into the lounge of Elsa's home. There she was placed on the settee and Elsa left the room hurriedly to get sal volatile and sponge and cold water.

'Excellent work, Brendy,' Castle murmured to his daughter. 'No wonder you are in such demand in your amateur dramatics group — In a moment or two, my dear,' he added to his wife, 'you may begin to recover gracefully — and don't forget your act. Everything depends on it. Later, you can remove that matt-white powder which gives you so much in common with a cadaver.'

The 'unconscious' Mrs. Castle gave a quick nod and became still again as Elsa came back into the room. By degrees, and appearing suitably bemused, Edith Castle drifted back to awareness and held her forehead tightly.

'What — ? Where . . . ?' she asked in puzzlement. 'Adam! Where are we?'

'In the home of this generous young lady,' Castle answered, nodding to Elsa as she smiled faintly. 'This is Miss Farraday — She came to our help after the smash.'

'Smash?' Mrs. Castle repeated in bewilderment; then she seemed to remember. 'Oh, of course! The car! You drove into something, didn't you?'

'A telegraph pole, my dear,' Castle agreed sadly. 'I assure you that it must have been a stone or something which hit the front wheel — You've been unconscious,' he hurried on. 'How are you? How do you feel? Anything hurting?'

His wife moved experimentally, helped by Brenda. Then as she tried to rise she fell back wincing.

'Something — low down on my back,' she said, gasping a little. 'It hurts abominably.'

Castle glanced about him worriedly as he heaved to his feet.

'Have you a 'phone, Miss Farraday? I must call a doctor — '

'I'm afraid I haven't,' Elsa apologized.

'Then where do I find a doctor? I must have him right away.'

'There's Dr. Phillips in the village high street. He's the only one around here.'

'I'll get him,' Brenda volunteered, 'even if I run all the way. I go to my left when I leave the gate, don't I, Miss Farraday?'

'That's right, and continue into the high street at the end of the lane,' Elsa instructed.

179

Brenda hesitated for a moment, realizing that the effort to perhaps get Elsa out of the house in order to direct the way had failed. She caught a slight nod from her father and dashed out, racing off down the front pathway.

'Just take it easy, my dear,' Dr. Castle advised. 'In case it is something internal and you disturb it . . . Oh, what a ghastly business this is!' he broke off in dismay. 'All of us on our way for a holiday down south — and now this! Really, Miss Farraday,' he added. 'You are most kind.'

'I'm only too glad to be of service,' she responded. 'Perhaps there is something I can get you? A drink of tea maybe?'

'That would be fine — ' Castle began; then he shook his head firmly. 'No. If something internal should be wrong a hot drink might cause serious damage. Thanks all the same.'

'But you can have one, surely — ? And your daughter too when she returns, Mr. — er — ?'

'I'm so sorry,' Castle apologized. 'Confused, you know. The name's Bennington. I'm Adam Bennington and this is my wife Edith. The youngster is Brenda, as you've probably gathered.'

'Yes.' Elsa nodded and smiled again. 'Well, you just lie still, Mrs. Bennington, and I'll see about some tea for us. I don't suppose the doctor will be long.'

Elsa went from the room again and Castle removed a silk handkerchief from his untidy lounge suit. It was an oldish one he was wearing, especially for the occasion. He mopped his cherubic face gently.

'So far, so good,' he breathed. 'Your acting is worthy of an Oscar, my dear.'

'At the moment, maybe,' she murmured, 'but what happens when the doctor gets here? I shan't be able to fool *him*!'

'My dear, as a psychologist you can take it from me that the patient can fool the doctor — especially a rustic one as he will be — any time he or she wishes. You can describe your symptoms; he can assume what is causing them. How does he know what is going on inside unless he has X-ray photographs? Leave it to me to help you if you get in a jam. He'll fix you up with a nice ailment to keep you here, unless I'm mistaken.'

'You get on the strangest cases, Adam!'

'Yes, don't I? And I always find you so co-operative — not forgetting Junior,' he added, with a little chuckle.

Saying no more he glanced about the room pensively, and almost immediately his gaze settled on the door with the eight shiny-headed screws driven into it. For a full half minute he considered it and then be murmured:

'So that's what Calthorp meant! Most interesting!'

His wife glanced at him and half started to asked a question, then she stopped as Elsa reappeared pushing a tea trolley. Castle studied her in that queer, detached way he had, summing her up in detail whilst appearing not to be taking any particular notice of her. Photographically he sized up her youthful figure, the quietness of her expression, the steadiness of her gray eyes. The dark afternoon frock she was wearing seemed, if anything, to make her appear even more receding.

'You are sure you won't try some tea,

Mrs. Bennington?' she asked, as she poured it out.

'I'd love to, but — Well, maybe my husband knows best.' Mrs. Castle gave a convincing little gasp as she moved slightly. Elsa looked at her for a moment and then handed a cup of tea to the huge psychiatrist.

'I feel,' he said, sitting down again and holding the cup with his little finger pointing obliquely, 'that we are a dreadful nuisance, Miss Farraday. The moment we know how my wife is we'll be on our way again.'

'There's no hurry,' Elsa assured him, settling in the armchair with teacup in hand. 'And in what do you propose to move? Surely not that car you've wrecked — ? And I'm afraid I haven't one which I can loan you.'

Castle gave a start. 'Great heavens, I'd forgotten all about the car! I'll have to 'phone — I mean get in touch with a garage. I'll send Brenda the moment she gets back.'

'Really, Adam, you're rather hard on the child,' his wife protested, languidly.

'She was involved in the accident as much as we were, remember. She must be in need of a few moments' rest instead of tearing about in this blazing sun.'

'At sixteen? Nonsense!' Castle said. 'Besides, I want us to be on the move as quickly as possible. We have trespassed on this young lady's good nature too much already . . . '

'Please don't think that,' Elsa interrupted. 'I'm only too glad of the company. I don't get many callers, you see, and for strangers to drop in — even if it is somewhat precipitately — makes quite a welcome change.'

'Oh, well then . . . ' Castle shrugged his fleshy shoulders. 'Maybe Brenda should rest a few minutes when she returns. Yes,' he added, thinking and considering his teacup, 'I suppose it is lonely here. You live quite on your own, Miss Farraday?'

'Yes.' Elsa looked at him absently for a moment and then added, 'Of late, though, I seem to have attracted attention — unwittingly. You may have noticed from the newspapers that I'm mixed up with the disappearance of a Chelsea artist.'

Castle smiled blandly. 'Are you really? Frankly, Miss Farraday, I wouldn't know. I don't read newspapers much: too full of crimes, threats of war, and the sordid side of life. I prefer to consider the bright side.'

'I can understand that,' Elsa replied, surveying his immense size and — though he was looking worried to conform to the occasion — the unmistakably genial lines of his face. 'I think it must be a great gift, to be able to always look on the bright side and enjoy it. I seem to be quite incapable of it.'

'I suppose some people are,' Castle admitted, and, typically, he did not advance any further. Though the way was wide open for him to develop the topic and even extract information from the girl, he refrained. That was never his way. He had the gift of sliding unnoticed into a person's inmost consciousness and seeming sublimely disinterested whilst doing it.

'Here's your daughter and the doctor,'

Elsa exclaimed suddenly, getting up as she glanced towards the front windows — and simultaneously there was the sound of car brakes.

She opened the front door and Brenda Castle came blundering into the lounge with all the gracelessness of sixteen, followed by a tall middle-aged, dour-faced G.P. He nodded to Elsa, with whom he was evidently acquainted; then at Castle's beckoning hand he drew up a chair and settled beside Mrs. Castle.

Castle watched broodingly, then glanced inquiry as the doctor finally stood up after having listened to Edith Castle's recital concerning her ailment.

'I can't tell exactly what the trouble is without a complete examination,' the doctor said, 'but I'm sure it's nothing alarming. Mostly the outcome of shock, I imagine. Reaction in the legs is normal and reflexes seem to be all right. Since there are no head injuries I suppose it was the shock of the impact which caused you to faint, madam?'

'She saw what was coming,' Castle answered for her. 'That, and the actual smash, frightened her severely, I'm afraid.'

'I see . . .'

'Perhaps her back trouble is only a wrench in the lumbar region,' Castle suggested. 'It's not uncommon . . .'

Judging from his expression Dr. Phillips did not like being taught his business, but just the same he nodded.

'Very probably. One of the most common injuries, in fact, when the body is suddenly and violently twisted as in a car smash. While it is not serious in itself it is capable of causing a good deal of inconvenience to the sufferer for a few days until it wears off.'

'A few days?' the psychiatrist repeated. 'But — but you don't mean that my wife can't be on her way in an hour or two?'

'My dear sir, if your wife moves about in her present overstrained condition I won't be responsible,' the doctor said grimly. 'What is more I would like to make a more thorough examination if the condition does not clear up. Can't afford to take chances with these things.'

Castle fondled his chins. 'Well, if you

say so that is as it must be, I suppose. I must find a taxi from somewhere and have her carried to it. Then maybe we can put up at an hotel in the village.'

'You are giving yourself a great deal of unnecessary worry, Mr. Bennington,' Elsa said, after a moment. 'There are two spare rooms in this house which I can soon put to rights for your wife and yourself — and Brenda. You mustn't think of letting your wife journey about, even in a taxi, until she is a good deal better.'

'But — '

'That's very generous of you, Miss Farraday,' the doctor said. 'I'll be here tomorrow for a further look at you, Mrs. Bennington. Good day.'

He turned and began to hurry out, obviously a busy man — then Castle called after him.

'Just a moment, doctor! Would you mind giving my daughter a lift as far as the village? I want her to find a garage and have my car removed.'

'Pleasure,' the G.P. assented, and Brenda hurried after him.

Elsa closed the front door and then

came back slowly into the lounge.

'I think I'll have that cup of tea now,' Mrs. Castle said quietly, biting her lip as her husband helped her into a half-sitting, half-lying position. 'Evidently it won't do me any harm.' Elsa poured it out and handed it to her, then she caught Castle's look.

'We're all deeply grateful to you for your help, Miss Farraday,' he said quietly. 'And naturally I must insist on paying for every hour we are here — '

'There's really no necessity.'

'Maybe not, but I insist on it. We would not expect to walk into an hotel and live on their generosity, so there's no reason why we should do so here. Believe me, we'll move on the moment my wife is fit. Maybe later tomorrow.'

'It's of no consequence,' Elsa said, shrugging. 'As I told you, I have very few callers and I like company . . . of the right kind. You can stay as long as ever necessary.'

'Brenda shall help you all she can,' Mrs. Castle decided. 'It will share the work. It's far more difficult to cater for four than for one.'

'Well, all right,' Elsa agreed, smiling; then she seemed to think of something and her expression changed a little. The smile faded. She said slowly: 'If by some chance I should receive a visit from the police, and in consequence have to leave home, we will discuss further. I think you should know that that is a possibility.'

'It all sounds most grim, Miss Farraday,' Castle commented, frowning.

'It is,' she sighed. 'I wouldn't have mentioned it at all, but since you may be here for a day or two I don't wish you to have the sudden unpleasant surprise of finding the police here talking to me without you knowing what it is all about. You are quite sure you haven't seen the newspapers?' she asked, a trifle incredulously.

'I have,' Mrs. Castle said, and gave a serious smile. 'But the papers say such things, don't they? The incredible part to me is that we happened to land in the very house of the woman in the case. It's a small world, isn't it?'

'I don't know much about it,' Castle

said calmly. 'What's supposed to have happened, anyway?'

'Apparently a young artist by the name of — er — Hexley has disappeared, Adam,' his wife told him. 'A Miss Farraday — *this* Miss Farraday, extraordinarily enough — was engaged to him, and she, and several other people are being badgered by the police for information. That's all there seems to be in it when the sensational garnishings are removed . . . Am I not right, Miss Farraday?'

'Quite right. At least,' Elsa said, 'you have some idea of the person I seem to be — according to the newspapers. I assure you I am not like that really. It's all a most dreadful business, and I still haven't the remotest idea how it will end.'

'My wife and I take people as we find them,' Castle assured her, smiling. 'If the police should come here bothering you we will at least know why, and I might be able to help you too, come to think of it.'

Elsa looked at him with interest. 'You might? How?'

'I am a lawyer,' Castle said, and breathing hard he fished in his jacket pocket and drew forth a visiting card, one of a batch which he had had printed the previous day. Elsa took it and read:

Adam Bennington
Barrister-at-Law
Vance Chambers
Middle Temple
London

Castle watched the girl in silence. Vance Chambers were occupied by one of his greatest friends, a Q.C., who would be ready for anything that might happen should Elsa take it into her head to make inquiry.

'That's fine,' Elsa said, looking up and smiling. 'I feel quite at home now in admitting my troubles. A lawyer is so like a doctor, don't you think?'

'Very much so,' Castle agreed, with a touch of dryness. 'However, bear it in mind, and if you need legal advice I'll gladly give it, if only to repay you for your kindness.'

He seemed about to say more and then changed his mind at a vigorous banging on the front door. It was the energetic Brenda, and accompanying her was a greasy-looking individual in blue overalls.

'I got him, dad,' Brenda exclaimed, bouncing in. 'He'll tell you himself.'

'Afternoon, sir,' the mechanic said, and dumped the car's luggage, comprising two suitcases, on the floor. 'Afternoon, Miss Farraday . . . About the car, sir; it's in a mess, I'm afraid.'

'Yes,' Castle agreed gravely, 'I'm afraid it is. Anyway, what can you do about it?'

'Tow it to the garage and find out how much is needed to patch it up — and from the look of it there'll be plenty. Engine's pretty well wrecked, I'm afraid.'

'I have the feeling,' Castle sighed, 'that I shall have to buy a new car. All right,' he agreed. 'Thanks. I'll drop in tomorrow and see how you're going on.'

The man nodded and departed. A silence fell for a moment, each looking at the other, then Elsa said quietly:

'If you'd like to lie down in bed, Mrs. Bennington, I'll be glad to see what I can fix up for you.'

'No, no, thanks all the same,' Mrs.

Castle protested. 'That would make me feel far too much like an invalid. I'm sure I'll be all right here. I can rest my back comfortably.'

'Just as you like.' Elsa glanced at Castle, then at Brenda. 'You'll wish to freshen up. Come with me and I'll show you around.'

11

It was during the evening meal, Mrs. Castle having managed to 'struggle' as far as the table, when Brenda, briefed beforehand by her father, went into action. The conversation, which had been pursuing normal enough channels, suddenly changed its course as she said:

'I do wish I never had to grow up!'

Elsa looked at her in surprise. Castle did too, but it was only simulated. His blue eyes moved to Elsa, studying her expression.

'What an extraordinary thing to say!' Elsa exclaimed.

'It may seem so to you, Miss Farraday, but you're grown up,' Brenda responded. 'You've forgotten what childhood's like — and adolescence too, I expect. I don't ever want to grow up because it will mean taking over responsibilities and losing many of the things which make youth worth while.'

'Rather contrary to some of the remarks I've heard from young folk of your age, Brendy,' Castle commented, smiling expansively. 'Many young people are glad to grow out of childhood because they feel that in so doing they can fight for themselves, on equal terms with the grown-ups. As children and adolescents they stand no chance.'

'How very, very true,' Elsa agreed, gazing absently in front of her.

Castle gave her a glance and moved another man on his mental chessboard.

'You have had experience of such young people, Miss Farraday?'

'Yes — indeed I have!' The girl's lips tightened for a moment. 'Myself, for instance. I had parents who were mercilessly strict. I was not allowed any freedom, and I had to tolerate their undoubtedly brutal treatment because I was too young to fight back. I only found liberty when they died.'

'You are sure you didn't find it before then?' Castle murmured, and the girl gave him a sharp look.

'How could I?'

The psychiatrist chuckled. 'Well, in the course of meeting many repressed young folk, the natural outcome of my profession as a lawyer, I have always noticed that they have found an outlet somehow. They just have to, you see. Nature won't permit herself to be restrained indefinitely. I think there must have been some way in which you found liberty, Miss Farraday, though perhaps it was only in your imagination.'

'Well, I did take to writing stories,' she admitted.

Castle spread his hands. 'There we are! What did I tell you? I'll wager that you wrote romances, if only to satisfy the void that was in your adolescent heart.'

'No.' Elsa's dark head shook. 'I wrote, and still write, thrillers. Crime stories. And for years I had no success, chiefly because I had to be so secretive. Then shortly after my parents died two years ago I began to get acceptances. Now I'm quite well known.'

'Splendid! Thrillers, eh? What in the world turned you to writing crime stories of all things?'

Elsa hesitated, then with a slow setting of her mouth she answered:

'I enjoyed inflicting on imaginary people something of the unhappiness which had been inflicted on me, from babyhood up. I suppose that sounds pretty diabolical, but it's the truth. I — I sort of felt that in that way I was getting my own back.'

Castle fondled his chins and contemplated the table.

'It is said, of course, that much of a writer is in his or her works. Maybe that is why your books are successful, Miss Farraday: there is so much in them based on bitter experience.'

'If you ever read any — or have read any,' Elsa said, 'please don't think that *everything* I put into them bears a real-life relationship. Otherwise you'll get the impression that I've spent my life in a medieval dungeon, or something!'

Mrs. Castle gave a smile and Brenda giggled openly — but Dr. Castle did neither. He played idly with the napkin ring beside him.

'I am a voracious reader of novels, even

though I detest newspapers,' he said, after a moment, 'and I consume thrillers by the truckload, but I can't recall the name Farraday anywhere. I take it you use a pseudonym?'

'Yes — Hardy Strong. I found a man's name moved me to the top quicker than anything.'

'You chose a nice, dominating one,' Castle commented. 'And I'd like the chance to read some of these thrillers of yours. You have some by you, I suppose?'

'Oh, yes — a copy of every one I've written.' Elsa got to her feet. 'Why don't you come and see my study and choose whichever book you'd like? In fact all of you might like to see where I work?'

'I would!' Brenda exclaimed, jumping up actively.

'Excellent idea.' Castle struggled to his feet, breathing hard, and then helped up his wife. She made several wry expressions and held her back painfully as he helped her slowly from the room.

'I suppose I shouldn't be doing this,' she said, 'but I'm a firm believer in defeating any physical ailment by trying to carry on as usual.'

Elsa gave an understanding nod and waited until she and Castle had reached her at the door, then she led the way across the hall and into her study. She switched on the lights to dispel the lowering evening twilight.

'What a lovely, quiet little room!' Brenda exclaimed in delight, glancing about her. 'Is that where you work, Miss Farraday — at that table in the window?'

Elsa nodded silently and Brenda glanced again at the disordered mass of blank and written quarto sheets; then with her mother and father she turned to the massive bookcase as Elsa motioned to it.

'Ah yes, indeed,' Castle murmured, considering a row of titles. 'Obviously you are a prolific writer, Miss Farraday.'

He did not add that he had read three of the books in the brief time he had had before arriving here by 'accident.' With every sign of interest he selected the novels one by one and glanced through them. Elsa stood watching him, her brows knitted.

'Yes indeed,' Castle repeated, beaming as he glanced up. 'These appear to be just the kind of thing I like, Miss Farraday. No trimmings — the plain, unvarnished tough facts. That's the stuff!'

'Apparently my public is impressed too,' Elsa responded. 'To judge from the royalty returns, that is. But those who know me personally tell me they're frightful.'

'Why?' Castle looked surprised.

'They seem to think the stories are brutal and sordid — grim stuff even if a man had written them, but when they realize that *I* did them they're nearly shocked out of their senses.'

'Then they're squeamish!' Castle declared. 'I've only glanced, of course, but I can see that you know your job.' He took one of the books, slipped it in his jacket pocket, and then closed the bookcase doors. Interested, he looked at the manuscript in course of execution on the dcsk. 'And this is how it looks in the 'building-up' stage, I take it? Authors fascinate me, you know.'

He picked up a sheet of the quarto idly and glanced through it. He read a couple of sentences pensively:

In the dak there was something she
had never sen before. It filled her with
a sudden and tremndous terror . . .

'My word,' he murmured. 'I thought I
held the prize for missing letters out of
words, but evidently you can teach me a
few tricks, Miss Farraday! Haste, I
suppose?'

She laughed. 'I'm afraid so. I've quite a
habit of missing letters out. I have all my
manuscripts retyped by an expert and she
straightens out the missing bits. I just
haven't got the time to write in full when
my thoughts are flowing freely.'

'No — of course not.' Castle studied
the handwriting, his mouth upturned at
the corners and his round, moonlike face
wearing no expression in particular.

The words in the handwriting were
executed in a series of short jerks, with
few of the letters properly connected.
Many of them, as he had already
remarked, were completely missing.

'Write anything else outside fiction?' he
inquired finally, putting the sheet down.

'No. Only thrillers. I don't find any

other form of fiction anything like as satisfying.'

'Mmmn. This type gives you a spacious feeling, I take it? A sort of sense of — er — superiority?'

'Funny you should say that,' Elsa replied in surprise. 'That is just what it does do, come to think of it.'

Castle did not say any more. The survey of the study over, Elsa led the way back into the lounge and Mrs. Castle was helped back to the settee. Whilst Castle stayed with her, his huge bulk deep in an armchair, Brenda offered her assistance in clearing away the dinner things and preparing the rooms that Elsa had to offer.

'We are learning things, my dear,' Castle murmured, when at last he and his wife were alone. 'Doubtless you are thinking that we are progressing nowhere — rapidly?'

'I'm not a psychiatrist, Adam,' she responded. 'But certainly I cannot see that we have discovered anything beyond the fact that Miss Farraday is quite a pleasant, good-natured young woman.'

Castle tugged out his long-stemmed, small-bowled pipe and filled it from an oilskin pouch.

'That young woman is extremely ill — mentally,' he commented, brooding, 'and she doesn't seem to realize it herself. It isn't guesswork,' he added, seeing his wife's quick, disbelieving glance. 'It stands out a mile in a number of places — and chiefly in her handwriting. I've seen writing like hers many a time — disjointed, and with letters left out. It is an established fact that people who leave letters out of their words without realizing it have a mental disturbance bothering them, though they are usually quite unaware of it and blame their omissions on lack of time. If it isn't stopped the trouble gets worse until finally . . . '

Castle stopped, lighted his pipe and puffed at it gently for a moment or two. Then he added, 'The writing itself, too. It belongs to a woman of exceptionally erratic character.'

'Do you mean,' Mrs. Castle asked slowly, with something like horror forming on her face, 'that you, Brendy, and I are shut up in this house with a . . . a killer?'

'We may be; but I don't think so. In any case I'm pretty sure that we shall never become objects of her attention. Her passion, as I see it, is only to cultivate those who can put her in the limelight, and we can't do that. Not in the way she would like it, at least.'

Mrs. Castle was plainly bewildered. 'Limelight? How do you mean? Why should a retiring girl like that want to — '

'That retiring pose, my dear, doesn't mean a thing,' Castle interrupted. 'It isn't the real Elsa Farraday. The real Elsa is an embittered, unhappy young woman, trying with everything that is in her to break free from fetters sealed on her in childhood. You heard her admit that she was mercilessly treated by her parents.'

'Yes, but surely she's outgrown that by now?'

'Very few people outgrow the experiences of childhood, especially if they be unhappy ones,' Castle answered seriously. 'I have not yet found out the full facts concerning her childhood, but I will before I've finished, and on that I hope to be able to base everything. As things stand now I can say with some certainty that what that young woman longs for more than anything else on earth is domination. But she wishes to achieve it in such a way that she herself is not presented to the populace.'

'How utterly contradictory!' Mrs. Castle said, thinking.

'Maybe, but not if you understand these things, as I do. She is frightened, I think, of the naked publicity which would involve her personally — so, to draw attention to herself, over which she can gloat in private, she resorts to other methods. For one thing, she writes: that brings her reflected glory whilst she herself can stay in retirement — unlike the actress who is on show and has to reveal her personality. Also on the dominant side we have the singular pen-name she has chosen . . . '

'Hardy Strong?'

'Exactly. Both words, in their literal sense, mean bold, audacious, robust. In other words — dominant. I'd like to wager that Miss Farraday gets a tremendous kick out of a name like that. It suggests power, something that she has never had throughout her life until perhaps now . . . Again, consider the case of Hexley, to whom she became engaged. It appears that as long as it was possible for him to paint her portrait, and so perhaps once again bring her a good deal of reflected glory, and once again without her needing to be present in person to do it, everything was all right. But the moment she knew he could not paint any more she cut him dead. His usefulness, as far as she was concerned, had ceased.'

'Yes, that does seem to hold together,' Mrs. Castle admitted; then after thinking for a moment she asked, 'Do you think, Adam, that she is trying to make it up to herself for the things she didn't get in her youth because of parental domination?'

'I'm perfectly sure of it, and it falls into onc exact class of mental ailment. I've much to do, though, before I'm sure which class it is . . . One thing is clear, her struggle to liberate herself is expressed through her novels, and the strange aberrations of her mind find reflection in the sordid cruelty of the stories she writes. As you know, yesterday I set myself to whizz through three of her novels. They are all of a pattern — brutal, yet brilliantly done. An imagination many would give anything to possess, but soured with her own innate sense of bitter injustices.'

'Then what do you propose to do next? You'll have to be careful how far you go, won't you, in case she starts suspecting that you're up to something.'

'There are two things I wish to do next — find out for myself what is behind that screwed door there' — Castle nodded to it — 'and also see that room of miniature furniture which Calthorp mentioned. Naturally, I'll be trespassing, and taking a risk, but it won't be for the first time. This young woman is an exceptionally interesting problem, and I hope I may be able to help her. Incidentally, it is noteworthy — according to Calthorp — that before she met Hexley Miss Farraday was thinking of becoming engaged to a local man, a commercial by the name of

Hargraves. Seems that when she cut with Hexley, Hargraves returned into the picture and asked her to become engaged to him. She refused, saying that there were reasons why she did not wish to get married then.'

'With so much hanging over her head in the Hexley case, that is hardly surprising, is it?'

'There might be the much greater reason that she hopes she may yet meet another man who can give her as much back-handed fame as Hexley could have done, a thought which had never occurred to her until she met him. Certainly she must realize that marrying Hargraves cannot advance her any. She has, so to speak, tasted blood, which makes her dissatisfied with ordinary prospects.'

Castle was not able to say any more at that moment for Elsa returned with Brenda beside her, and immediately the conversation turned into commonplace channels.

12

Timing himself to awaken at two in the morning, Dr. Castle did so to the minute. He smiled to himself at this achievement in self-discipline, noticed that his wife was sleeping peacefully, and then slid out of bed, as carefully as his immense bulk would allow. He succeeded, apparently, without creating disturbance.

In silence he partly dressed in shirt, trousers, and rubber-soled shoes — which he had put in his luggage against such an occasion as this — then making sure his flashlamp was working properly be slipped it in his pocket and glided silently from the room.

Closing the door gently he stood listening for a moment, but the house was deadly silent. From outside, too, there were no sounds in the expanses of countryside.

He went down the staircase, the thick carpet and rubber-soled shoes absorbing all noise — and so into the lounge. At the door with the shiny-headed screws down the sides he paused and fished a barrel-like tool from his pocket, containing screwdriver, corkscrew, small file, and other useful implements. Since Sergeant Dixon had already loosened the screws on the earlier occasion they now moved easily enough. In five minutes the psychiatrist had them all free and put them in his pocket.

Flashing his torch before him he went down into the cellar and looked about him. Where Calthorp had been looking for a body, Castle was looking for something quite different — evidences, bits in the puzzle, which would help him to form an even clearer picture of the mind of Elsa Farraday.

He prowled slowly, flashing the torch beam about him. When he reached the rusted iron door he stood considering it, then satisfied that it had not been budged for years he went further, pausing again at an ancient iron ring cemented deeply into one of the square blocks which formed the cellar wall.

Castle's expression changed a little.

The ring itself was only slightly rusty and had plainly been used up to a recent date for some purpose or other. The base of it, where it entered the stone, was flawed with red erosion.

'Mmm,' Castle murmured to himself. 'Pretty much as I'd thought — and what a story it tells!'

He turned away, wandering to the furthest corner of the dirty, coal-dust ridden basement. So grimed were the walls he almost missed what was actually an old cupboard door set into the wall. Returning to it he pulled it open, the glare of the torch beam settling on a solitary object coiled up like a snake and pushed at the extreme back of the lowest shelf.

Frowning to himself, Castle pulled the thing out. It uncoiled into a thick leather belt with a heavy brass buckle. Obviously it was a man's. Castle's mouth tautened as he glanced back towards the spot where the ring in the wall was situated, then he turned to a more minute examination of the belt, putting the torch close to it and throwing into relief curious grayish marks as though paint had been spattered from a wet brush.

'I hope I'm right,' he murmured.

From his pocket he took a penknife and an old envelope. With infinite care he scraped the powdery substance away in a fine film until he had a fair deposit. Then he sealed the envelope, folded it four times, and put it in his wallet. The belt he carefully recoiled and replaced exactly in the circle of dust where he had found it. He was satisfied that Elsa Farraday would never come and look for it — but if by some chance she did he felt sure she would never realize the belt had been moved.

'Which seems to be that,' Castle told himself, and returned silently to the lounge.

He spent another five minutes re-screwing the door — then he glided from the lounge into the kitchen and looked about him. At the sight of the screwed cupboard doors he smiled faintly to himself but did not touch them. Departing, he went in the same ghostlike silence up the staircase, glided past the bedrooms, and paused at the door over the hall. He did not go into action immediately. For some time he remained lounging by the door, listening for the least sign of a noise. Since there was none he finally moved, tested the door and, as he had expected, found it locked.

With the master-key he carried he had no difficulty in turning the lock: there was nothing very complicated about it, anyway. It slid back gently and he eased his ponderous bulk into the room beyond, locking the door on the inside. Breathing musically he switched on the torch and looked about him. Immediately he had something of the same sensation of Gulliver in Lilliput that Barbara Vane had experienced when she had first stepped into this room.

Nowhere, as he moved about noiselessly, did Castle find a piece of furniture higher than his waist. Even the minute bookcase, the tallest piece of all, was no more than three feet six in height.

Fondling his chins he considered everything carefully, glancing finally at the normal window, fireplace, and lofty ceiling.

Then the wandering beam of his torch settled on what he had taken to be a second window. Going across to it he found that the curtains were covering a recess in which was a variety of children's frocks. In the base of this hanging wardrobe were neat shoes from patent leather to feather-edged bedroom shoes.

'Curiouser and curiouser,' he mumured. 'In fact there is a distinct Alice in Wonderland aspect about this whole business . . . '

With some effort he went down on his knees and explored the floor of the hanging wardrobe with more detail, smiling to himself when he came upon a series of oblong boxes piled one on top of the other. Raising the lids of each he found a fully dressed beautifully made doll looking up at him unblinkingly.

'Splendid!' he chuckled to himself. 'Absolutely splendid. Just as I had hoped.'

He straightened up again and stood puffing whilst he once again contemplated the room, then, satisfied there was nothing more which interested him he silently let himself out into the passage, locked the door behind him, and went downstairs again.

This time he went to the study, nor was it locked. Torch in hand he moved to the desk where the quarto sheets were still lying as they had been earlier in the evening. He picked them up, found the written ones were more or less numerically in order, and finding they had only gone as far as page thirty he settled down in the armchair by the desk and began reading from the beginning, still using his torch and keeping his ear cocked for the slightest untoward sound.

The more he read the more absorbed he became, and one sentence in particular, remarkable — as was the whole manuscript — for its missing letters in the words, impressed him enough for him to read it over several times. Though he had no means of knowing it, it was the section that Barbara Vane had read and, at that time, it had marked the limit of the story's progress —

She knew that there could be no escape from such daming evidence, but at lest even from this complte destruction of her life she could extract one profund consolation — as a murderess she could achive that which, as an innocent, she had nevr achieved . . .

Carefully Castle copied down the extract in his notebook and then smiled to himself.

'And to think,' he muttered, 'that I was hoping I might find a diary lying about somewhere, when this brief statement is far more revealing than a diary could ever be. My word, it's the answer!'

He sat staring blankly before him, thinking, his interest in the remaindcr of the manuscript momentarily banished. After a while he returned to it and read through doggedly as far as the story had progressed, but nowhere else did he find any other section quite so interesting.

'Yes, self-revelation,' he murmured. 'Everybody ruled by an ego has some way of recording it, the most common being by a diary which, after death, is often found by others. The egomaniac has no other way of advertising to the world those actions which in life are kept secret . . . Mmm.'

He put the papers back in pretty much the same disorder as he had found them, then went silently from the room. He was complimenting himself on how subtly he had accomplished everything when his wife's voice in bed beside him made him start.

'Well, Adam, have you finished prowling yet?'

'Er — yes, my dear,' he admitted. 'But how did you know that I *had* been?'

Mrs. Castle laughed softly. 'Good heavens, Adam, you don't suppose that a baby Jumbo like you can get out of bed without shaking the whole room, do you? I've been lying here ever since you went, wondering what you might be up to.'

'Oh, you have?' Castle sighed. 'Well, I've been piecing together odd bits in the puzzle — as I said I was going to, and I have been remarkably successful, too.'

'In what way? Proving that Miss Farraday murdered that man Hexley?'

'No — proving that she didn't. I never did think that she did and now I'm convinced of it.'

There was a momentary silence in the dark room. 'Then who *did* kill him?'

'The way things are looking,' Castle murmured, 'I'm beginning to doubt if *anybody* did.'

'Suicide then? Because he knew he could never paint again?'

'No; not even that . . . ' Castle stifled a yawn and added, 'Don't ask me to explain more now, my dear. I've a lot of sleep on which to catch up. I'll tell you everything soon enough.' A long pause followed and then he added, 'There's one thing I am quite sure of, and it is that Miss Farraday must have been the most disappointed young woman in this world when Calthorp didn't arrest her on suspicion of murder.'

'Disappointed! Great heavens, I should think it must have been a tremendous relief.'

'Not for Miss Farraday. I read something tonight which satisfies me that that was the one thing she was hoping for — and it misfired.'

'Well, go on!' Mrs. Castle urged. 'Having got me this far you can't leave me hanging in mid-air. Why did she hope for that?'

'Because, and I quote from her manuscript — 'as a murderess she could achieve that which, as an innocent, she could never have achieved . . . ' Unquote. That achievement being notoriety, and notoriety is only fame tarnished with scandal. The public would have talked about her. She would have been noticed — as a murderess.'

'And, because she was not accused of murder you think that she must have been disappointed — because it meant she had failed in her object?' Mrs. Castle sighed. 'Well, Adam, you probably know what you mean, but I certainly don't. For instance, I cannot understand why she confessed to a murder at all when she must have known, especially as a thriller-writer, that she just couldn't be arrested without the body being produced.'

'She could have been arrested on *suspicion* though, body or no body, and that alone would have drawn immediate attention to her — but Calthorp did not do that Calthorp's a wary bird, and always has been. He wanted to be sure of his facts first. Arresting a person on suspicion and then finding them innocent is not a very good reflection on the police.'

'The whole business is weak somewhere!' Mrs. Castle declared. 'That girl, in spite of confession, must certainly know that her plan for achieving notoriety as a murderess can never be accomplished until the body is found. That being so, why on earth did she ever put the body in the swamp, as she seems to have done, when she must have been aware that that very act prevented it from being discovered?'

'The answer to that one, my dear, is that she planned to gain fame by being arrested and having all the sordid details published, and finally escape with her life because of the absence of a body by which she could be definitely charged. Certainly a risky way of achieving limelight, but evidently she knows that the swamp never gives up its victims. What spoiled things for her was Calthorp's decision not to arrest her.'

'I wish,' Mrs. Castle said thoughtfully, 'I could understand *why* she wants to achieve notice by every conceivable method.'

'She can't help herself. It's a natural reaction — but since it carries us some distance ahead of that which we have proved, I'll say no more — And I'm losing sleep.'

Castle didn't speak for several moments, then he murmured:

'One thing, my dear — Calthorp wondered if Miss Farraday was speaking the truth when she said that her father had screwed up that door in the lounge, and presumably the cupboard doors in the kitchen. It seemed to him that the screws were much too new to have been in for two years. And I think he's right. Those screws have not been there above two months or so, I'll wager.'

'Then *she* screwed them up? Whatever for?'

Dr. Castle did not respond. He was snoring gently.

★　★　★

The following morning, under her husband's orders, Mrs. Castle had her breakfast in bed, Brenda bringing it to her and Elsa appearing for a few moments to inquire as to her health.

'I can hardly move,' Mrs. Castle lied gracefully. 'I was so afraid this might happen after a night's rest.'

'The doctor will be back again this morning,' Elsa said, with her queer little smile. 'He'll soon see what can be done to set you right. In the meantime don't worry about a thing.'

'You're most kind, Miss Farraday,' Mrs. Castle told her.

Elsa said no more, leaving Brenda with her mother. She went downstairs to find Dr. Castle at the close of a breakfast that he had evidently gathered together for himself. He beamed on her as she came into the room.

'Ah, good morning, Miss Farraday! You won't mind my having rustled together a meal for myself, I trust?'

'Not at all,' the girl responded, shrugging. 'Whilst you are here, please feel at home.'

She stood beside the table for a moment and considered the toast, meat-paste, and marmalade that Castle had discovered for himself. She seemed to be deciding what she herself would eat. Castle munched daintily as he regarded her, then he said:

'I'm a little puzzled about something, Miss Farraday. The cupboards in the kitchen — To my surprise I found them screwed up.'

'Yes.' She gazed at him steadily. 'My father did that to stop them swinging. I've never unscrewed them since.'

Castle nodded but did not say any more. He had noted the matter-of-fact way in which the girl had responded, which suggested she was well prepared for the question; then concluding his breakfast he got to his feet.

'I take it there is a post office in the village, Miss Farraday?'

She nodded.

'Good. I'd better wire one or two of my friends and let them know what happened to us, otherwise they'll be wondering. Be a change from Brenda doing all the running about, and I daresay the exercise will do me good . . . '

With that he managed to escape before he had to explain himself further. Smiling thoughtfully he left the house a few minutes later, a rather small black homburg on his silvery hair and his nose sniffing appreciatively at the warm summer wind blowing across the fields.

When he reached the village post office he hesitated, fondling his chins and contemplating the sharp-nosed woman flitting about behind the assorted groceries and fly-blown confections.

'Won't do,' he muttered. 'In a place as small as this a registered letter to Scotland Yard would attract more attention than an earthquake. No, I'd better go further.'

He did — taking a bus fifteen miles to Guildford. Here he bought a registered envelope at the general post office and in one of the partitions reserved for writers of telegrams he wrote a brief note —

For forensic department to deal with by precipitin test for blood-group, report to be sent to Chief Inspector Calthorp. Adam Castle.

This done he addressed the envelope to Calthorp at Scotland Yard, obtained his receipt, and then went outside to a telephone kiosk. In a few moments he was speaking to Calthorp himself.

'Well, doc, I'm glad to hear from you!' Calthorp exclaimed. 'I was just beginning to wonder how you were getting on. From where are you speaking?'

'Guildford — safer than locally from Midhampton,' Castle went into a brief résumé of his audacious entry into Elsa Farraday's home and then continued: 'I've just mailed to you, registered, some grayish dust, Calthorp. My guess is that it's blood, but only the bendizine and precipitin tests will prove that. Get forensic to classify it and find out its group.'

'Easy enough, but how much good will it do us?'

'It should help to prove whether or not Miss Farraday was lying when she said she killed Clive Hexley.'

'Huh? How can it?'

'I'm not telling you that over the 'phone — too dangerous; but I wish you'd meet me this afternoon when you have that report through and we'll have a little conference. Say — Guildford railway station at three. How would that suit?'

'How do you expect the letter to reach me that quickly?'

'Express mail. You'll get it in under an hour.'

'That's different,' Calthorp said. 'Okay, I'll be there, if only to find out what I've missed.'

With that he rang off and Castle chuckled to himself. He squeezed out of the kiosk and wandered back thoughtfully towards the bus stop; then as he passed a florist's window he paused for a moment, turned back, and surveyed the floral offerings.

'Hmmm,' he mused. 'My word, yes! I

think somebody or other once said that to be natural is the surest way of winning a person's secrets . . . Or did I just think of it? Anyway, it's worth a try. What more natural than roses for an invalid?'

He lumbered into the shop, bought two-dozen red roses, and then came out again with them held like a posy in front of his capacious middle. With sublime disregard for the glances cast at him whilst in the bus he sat with the roses held before him — but during the journey his slowly creeping fingers had detected exactly where all the thorns were.

He was still smiling when he rang the bell at Tudor Cottage and Elsa herself admitted him.

'It's a lovely day, Mr. Bennington,' she commented, preceding him into the lounge. 'Just the day for getting a lot of writing done.'

'Don't you ever go out?' he asked her in surprise.

'Just for the sake of it? No. If I go out there has to be a purpose behind it, otherwise it always strikes me as a waste of time — But what lovely roses!' Elsa broke off, and for a moment real womanly appreciation of the magnificent blooms took possession of her.

'A dozen for you, my dear young lady, and a dozen for my wife,' Castle explained, beaming. 'I do so hope you'll accept — as a small token of appreciation for all you've done for us — '

'Well — '

'Of course you will,' Dr. Castle chuckled. 'Now, if you have some kind of vase?'

Elsa came forward to take the roses from him, and at the same moment he deliberately let them slip. Her reaction was as he had expected. She dived to save them, grabbed, as he too pulled upwards. Then she winced and shook her fingers sharply as little spots of blood appeared on them.

'Thorns?' Castle asked in concern. 'Oh, I'm so sorry, Miss Farraday! Here — let me help you.'

He dumped the roses on the table and with his handkerchief wiped away the blood spots. He found the girl looking at him seriously when at last he had desisted.

'They're only scratches,' she smiled. 'Nothing to worry about but they do sting for a moment — I'll soon fix these up for you.'

She gathered the roses, gingerly this time, and went with them into the kitchen. Castle stood pushing his handkerchief back into his pocket and smiling to himself; then he swung round at a sharp ringing on the front door.

'I'll go,' he called, as Elsa appeared in the kitchen doorway — and admitted the doctor.

'Morning,' the G.P. greeted, in his dour fashion. 'Any better news of your wife, Mr. Bennington?'

'I'm afraid not,' Castle sighed. 'Unless, that is, she has improved whilst I've been out. I haven't seen her for a couple of hours and at that time she was complaining that she could hardly move.'

'Well, we'll have a look. Morning, Miss Farraday,' the doctor added, as Elsa appeared with the roses equally divided into two glass vases.

Castle took one of them from her with a smile of thanks and followed the G.P. up the stairs. Just in time, as the door opened, Brenda and Mrs. Castle managed to look convincingly serious, and it was a striking contrast to the light-hearted conversation in which they had been indulging.

'Ah, good morning, Mrs. Castle.' Dr. Phillips' dourness relaxed into his bedside manner. 'And how are we?'

'Dreadfully stiff, I'm afraid,' Mrs. Castle told him,

'Mmm . . .' Phillips cocked an eye on Castle and, then Brenda.

'All right, we'll go,' the psychiatrist said, putting the roses on the table. 'For you, my dear,' he added, beaming.

'They're lovely, Adam! They really are!'

He nodded, took Brenda's arm, and led her out of the room. Out on the landing he winked at her solemnly.

'How much longer does this double crossing business go on, dad?' she whispered. 'I keep feeling that it's all dreadfully mean towards Miss Farraday — and that doctor too, if it comes to that.'

'There's a difference between meanness and strategy, Brendy,' Castle reproved her. 'Miss Farraday's actions have been anything but straight, so we have to fight her with the same weapons. As for the doctor, if his skill isn't equal to discovering that there is nothing whatever the matter with your mother — well, he deserves all that happens to him.'

'But we're not getting anywhere!' the girl protested, still keeping her voice low. 'Mother's told me about you wandering in and out of rooms in the night, and now you go off to buy her some roses. All very nice and pretty, but why doesn't something exciting happen?'

'What would you like — Miss Farraday brandishing a razor?' her father asked dryly.

'Of course not! But I do expect to see some kind of result!'

'You will, my dear, in time. I — ' Castle stopped and his expression became serious as the bedroom door clicked and Dr. Phillips reappeared. He snapped the second catch on his black bag and thought for a moment.

'Is it — bad?' Castle inquired gravely.

'Bad? Good heavens, no!' Phillips gave his leathery smile. 'As a matter of fact, Mr. Bennington, your wife, except for superficial stiffness of which she complains, has nothing the matter with her. The trouble yesterday must have been just a sprain. The stiffness should wear off by afternoon, especially when she starts to move about.'

'Oh, I see,' Castle nodded. 'Thanks very much.'

'Not at all. I shan't need to call again. I've left a bottle of liniment in the bedroom.'

'Much obliged, doctor — and send your account to me at Vance Chambers, Middle Temple, will you?' Castle called after him as he headed for the stairs.

Phillips gave an acknowledging salute and went on his way down the staircase. Evidently Elsa had been waiting — and listening — in the hall for her voice came floating up.

'I'm so glad Mrs. Bennington is so much better, doctor.'

'No doubt of it. Another few hours and

she'll be skipping around like you or I
. . . Good day, Miss Farraday.'

The front door closed and since Elsa
did not come up the stairs she had
evidently gone either to the lounge or the
study. Brenda Castle gave her father a
troubled look.

'Unless I have the idea wrong, dad,
that's pulled our cork,' she sighed. 'We've
no longer any excuse for staying here.'

Castle grinned. 'Oh, don't let that
worry you. As a matter of fact I've got all
I want out of this place.'

He opened the bedroom door and
followed the girl in; then he stood looking
at his wife benignly. She averted her eyes.

'I'm terribly sorry, Adam, but I did all I
could to convince the doctor that I'm ill.
He just wouldn't have any.'

'Which shows he's a better man than
I'd thought,' Castle commented. 'However, don't let it worry you. I'd guessed
that he would probably not be fooled
beyond this morning, which was why I
crammed all my investigating into one
night . . . We'll have to be on our way,
that's all. And Brendy, see if the passage

234

outside is empty.'

Brenda tiptoed swiftly to the door, opened it, and glanced outside. She closed it again and returned to the bedside with her thumb upturned significantly.

'To keep up appearances, my dear,' Castle resumed, sitting on the bed edge beside his wife so that the mattress springs creaked, 'We shall have to move on. I don't want Miss Farraday to suspect for one moment that we are not all we seem to be. I have everything I need here, so you had better start making so-called attempts to crawl about, gradually improving as time goes on. By five o'clock this afternoon you will be quite fit to travel.'

'To where?' Brenda asked.

'London. We're going back home. After lunch I shall depart, ostensibly in search of a car I can hire. I'll find one all right and come back for you in it whilst you, Brendy, in the interval will do the packing. Whilst I am searching for the car I shall also meet Chief Inspector Calthorp in Guildford: I've already made an appointment over the 'phone.'

Brenda rubbed her hands and, her blue eyes glowed with expectancy.

'Then we'll start to see something, eh Dad? You'll bring the chief back here with you and — '

'I shall do nothing of the kind,' Castle interrupted her calmly. 'I am merely meeting Calthorp in order that I may exchange notes — and had I known I was returning to London I would have left it over until then. However, it's too late now to telephone and stop him so I'll go through with it.'

He got up from the bed and his wife rose several inches higher to the horizontal.

'Brendy and I will go downstairs and tell Miss Farraday that we're departing today,' he said. 'You start to 'stagger' about, my dear — that is if you feel strong enough after the long rest in bed you've had!'

13

At three o'clock that afternoon, according to plan, Dr. Castle was at Guildford railway station and he and the Chief Inspector retired immediately to the nearest café and there began conversation over the coffee and cakes.

'That powdered stuff you sent was blood,' Calthorp said, his lean face grim. 'And it's group A-B. The age of it is about five years.'

'Mmm.' Castle contemplated a chocolate eclair longingly and then steeled himself and took a plain bun instead. 'That's what I'd hoped for. From it we may draw a certain significance.'

'So you inferred over the 'phone, but since you haven't yet told me where the stuff came from I can't see what you're getting at. I suppose it belongs to something which Hexley owned?'

'No, I think it is Miss Farraday's blood,' Castle answered quietly. 'The blood on that handbag, with which she struck Hexley — so she said — was group A-B: that you have proved. This new stuff is also A-B. Had it been any other group but that rare one, I would have accepted the possibility of coincidence, but as things are I just can't.'

'In other words, you are suggesting that that blood on the handbag was not Hexley's but Miss Farraday's?'

'Exactly, and in a way it is what I had expected, considering what I've found out about her.'

Calthorp frowned. 'But how did you get hold of this five-year old blood deposit?'

'I found it on a heavy belt in the basement, pushed away in a cupboard and forgotten. At some time, Calthorp, evidently five years ago according to forensic, I think that girl was mercilessly thrashed with that belt. What is more, I believe she was often shut up in that dark basement, fastened to an iron ring in the wall. That much I deduced from the ring being still fairly free of rust, from something scraping it — a rope or chain maybe — whereas everything else is corroding with rust. The blows with the belt were probably inflicted with such savagery that they drew blood, which of course got on to the belt.'

'Sounds logical,' Calthorp agreed. 'But at that time Miss Farraday must have been around twenty. Why on earth did she stand for such treatment? Why didn't she go to the police, run away, or do *something*? She's not a fool.'

'Let me ask you something,' Castle suggested. 'And answer it truthfully. If you had parents who were brutally strict, even cruel, and you were not naturally an audacious, courageous person, wouldn't you obey their orders as much when grown up as when a child?'

'Well — maybe,' Calthorp answered dubiously.

'You *would*!' Castle assured him. 'It is that which we learn in childhood which forms us as adults. It is then that the shapeless clay is fashioned for good or ill. It is then that the criminals and repressive types, and the men and women of vision, are created. Childhood and environment:

those are the key factors. So, then, let us consider Miss Farraday . . . '

Castle munched, the bun and took another drink of coffee before continuing:

'Miss Farraday suffers in an extreme form from something which we all have in one way or another — inferiority complex. It is a condition brought on in its severest state by a childhood of unrelieved brutality. I've learned enough from Miss Farraday to know that her parents treated her exceedingly badly, and in that lonely house, miles from anywhere, they could get away with it. This ill-treatment, I think, continued until she reached twenty-three — then they died — and she was too cowed and afraid of them to expose the business . . .

'But Nature had to strike a balance somewhere. Her individuality couldn't be completely smothered because, deep down, there is a glowing fire within her. She sought refuge, as most repressed folk do, in her imagination. She became a writer, and — as she quite freely admitted to me — she made imaginary people suffer all that she had suffered herself, thereby relieving something of the enormous mental and physical strain she was enduring.'

Calthorp lighted a cigarette and regarded Castle broodingly through the smoke.

'Okay, doc, it makes sense so far. Carry on.'

'Dominant in her mind were two things she had never enjoyed, or even glimpsed,' Castle continued, pondering. 'One was the carefree irresponsibility of a normal child; and the other was dominance — this latter quality only developing when she realized she was an adult and had had no chance of proving it to the world. So what did she do when she realized that, suddenly, parental cruelty had gone? That she was alone in the world with nothing but the memory of bitter, pitiless years? She became, at intervals, the child she had always wanted to be — '

'The miniature furniture!' Calthorp exclaimed, snapping his fingers. 'That what you mean?'

'That's just what I mean. My guess is that when she knew she was free she went and bought all the small furniture somewhere, and the children's clothes. Then at intervals — even to playing with dolls — she became a child, behaved as a child, and during such periods no doubt thought as a child. She was catching up on the carefree years she should have had. As for the financial cost of the furniture and the house itself, I assume she made it from her books. *But* — '

Dr. Castle paused, and raised a plump finger to emphasize. 'But, Calthorp, her normal adult mind was also at work, struggling for domination. Hence the small furniture. She had, if you grasp the idea, to dominate — to be bigger than everything else around her. In that way her superiority and childish instincts were both satisfied at the same time . . .

'Her longing for superiority also led her to choose the tough name of 'Hardy Strong' for her pseudonym on her books, which after the removal of her parents blossomed from frenzied secret scribbling into publishable stuff. But even that didn't satisfy her — Her upbringing had made her afraid of drawing attention to herself, and yet she wanted to gain attention. As a writer she could do that and keep the world at bay as well. As the subject of an Academy painting she could also achieve it — and still hold the public at arm's length. To my mind, nothing showed her inferiority complex more clearly than her abrupt breaking of the engagement when she knew that Clive Hexley could never bring her the reflected glory she had expected.'

Castle pulled out his pipe, lighted it, and continued.

'Hexley's failure to provide that which she had expected must have left an awful void in her mind — a vast, unsatisfied longing. So she chose yet another means of drawing attention to herself — still driven, mind you, by the urge to appear dominant in every situation. She tried to get herself arrested for the murder of Hexley, even though — had it come off — it would have meant that she herself was the direct target instead of it being reflected fame. Which gives us the measure of her desperate desire to achieve notice.

'She had hoped that you would arrest her on suspicion, which would have given her notoriety. She knew you could never actually accuse her of murder without producing the body. Cleverly, she did not admit her supposed guilt all at once. She waited for an opportunity and let you suspect other people as well to commence with — then when she was ready she made a 'confession.' It struck me as being completely unconvincing that her reason for confessing was to stop you looking at her room with the miniature furniture. That, I think, was merely a very weak excuse but the best one she could manage as a lever to make her confession seem as though it were being *forced* out of her. So . . . Well, you know what she said.'

'Then it's her blood on the bag? But what about the hair? That was certainly Hexley's. Where did it come from?'

'I don't know,' Castle answered broodingly. 'And of course there is still the chance that Hexley also had A-B blood group, though it's a long coincidence. Until we find a sample of Hexley's blood we can never prove our point — and how we're to find that Lord knows! But believe me, if we *can* find it and prove it to be different from that on the bag, and then confront Miss Farraday with the fact, I'll gamble she'll break down and tell everything before I'm finished with her.'

Through an interval Calthorp sat smoking pensively; then he said.

'Concerning this blood-grouping business. Because you found the belt with blood streaks on it, doesn't say it was because Miss Farraday was the victim. It could have been somebody else. Or even, since she seems to have such a queer nature, it could have been she who wielded the belt on somebody else.'

'Never in this world,' Castle answered quietly. 'Make no mistake, Calthorp, that girl is the quiet type, striving to gain attention by the least flamboyant method possible. She's not a sadist, though I admit that her desire to achieve domination in some form or other might lead her to extremes before she's finished. I agree that I have not proved it is her blood on the belt, but I think we can . . . For instance — '

245

He put his hand in his jacket pocket and withdrew a neatly folded handkerchief in a transparent envelope. Placing it on the table he pointed to it.

'Blood spots,' he explained. 'Get them analyzed. I know they belong to Miss Farraday because they're from some thorn stabs I — er — devised this morning. She hadn't the least idea that it was a trick. If *that* proves to be group A-B as well I think we can safely assume that the stains on the handbag and the belt are also hers. As to the hair, which is Hexley's — I just don't know.'

'You certainly have an unorthodox way of getting results,' Calthorp commented, pushing the cellophane bag and handkerchief into his pocket. 'I'll have the stains analyzed the moment I get back to the Yard. How do I let you know the result?'

'Come to my home. I'm returning to London this evening. I can't stay at Tudor Cottage any longer because there's no legitimate reason. Tell me something,' Castle added, 'how did Miss Farraday react when you told her you were going to explore the basement?'

'She raised no objections.'

'I'll wager one thing, Calthorp: she didn't come with you.'

'No. As a matter of fact she didn't I asked her to because I had the fear that she might slam the door on Dixon and me and screw it up. She didn't though. She just stood looking out on to the back garden — '

'Ah!' Castle interrupted, his blue eyes gleaming. 'Her back was to you, was it?'

'Uh-huh.'

'And whilst that basement door was open did she turn once and speak to you?'

'Er — no,' Calthorp responded, thinking. 'She only turned when Dixon had slammed the door shut.'

'Exactly!' Castle rubbed his podgy hands in delight. 'Just a little more evidence, Calthorp, which shows her mental reaction to that basement — and indeed to all places which are dark and suggest imprisonment. That is one reason why I had no qualms about disturbing that belt. I knew she would never come and look on the 'torture' chamber without some very compelling reason. It is simply a case of her not having the courage to look on the source of her childhood terrors. For the same reason she screwed up the big cupboard doors in the kitchen. There's a touch of claustro-phobia there, allied to her inferiority complex.'

Calthorp nodded but he did not say anything. It was clear he was not altogether at home with the psychiatrist's elucidation of mental foibles. Facts, understandable to the layman, were the only things that really interested the chief inspector. The realm of mental analysis had always seemed to him like so much mumbo-jumbo

'Usually,' Castle said, relighting his pipe, 'people of Miss Farraday's type keep a diary, record their voices, or otherwise make a history of their actions. Since they cannot reveal their activities openly to anybody else they satisfy their ego by writing about them. I had hoped whilst at Tudor Cottage to find a diary or some such thing but I found something infinitely better — a manuscript of a novel in the process of being written by Miss Farraday. Shorn of its external trimmings it amounts to a somewhat exaggerated version of her own activities, her way of recording what she had done, and one particular extract is outstanding. I copied it down and here it is . . . '

Calthorp took the slip of paper and frowned over it.

' 'As a murderess she could achieve that which, as an innocent she could never have achieved',' he repeated slowly. 'I think I see what you mean, doc. It's a reflection of herself — *she* trying to attract attention by seeming to be a murderess.'

'Just so — which you spoilt for her by not arresting her.'

'Nor shall I until I find the body; and between ourselves I haven't much hope of doing that.' Calthorp looked at the note again and puzzled for a moment. 'You slipping?' he inquired. 'Why all these mis-spellings?'

'That is exactly as Miss Farraday wrote the statement,' Castle responded calmly.

'And I surely don't have to tell you that words which have letters missed out are a sign of a peculiar twist in the writer's mind?'

'Says Hans Gross,' Calthorp smiled. 'Got it all tied up, haven't you?'

'The writing itself is also that of a person of peculiar mental tendencies,' Castle added. 'Tied up?' he repeated. 'Well — partly. I'm worried as to how to prove Hexley's blood-group. I find it an intolerable situation not to be able to find just that, and to be sure that it *is* his group. Once find the weak link in Miss Farraday's confession and I know we'll find out what really happened to Hexley.'

'Just what do you think did happen to him?' Calthorp asked, putting the note in his wallet for future study. 'I have thought of all the angles, including suicide, but I come right back to thinking of murder — not necessarily by Miss Farraday, for indeed I think less of her as the culprit than I ever did — but by somebody. Hargraves, maybe, or Terry Draycott, or — remotely — Miss Vane. But I'm well aware that I'll have the hell of a time proving it in regard to the last two, though I might be able to find something against Hargraves since his alibi isn't watertight in places. There are gaps in his activities where he could have got up to mischief.'

'For myself,' Castle said slowly; 'I have the feeling that murder cannot be laid specifically at the door of anybody. I have a vague theory forming as to what really might have happened to Hexley, and if I'm right it is the exact opposite of what has appeared to be the case so far. That I can only prove — I hope — as I go along.'

He reflected further and then glanced at his watch. Immediately he struggled to his feet.

'My word, Calthorp, I must be going! I've a car to hire yet and then get back to Midhampton for the wife and Brendy. Contact me in London and we'll decide then what to do next.'

Calthorp nodded, rose also, and accompanied him across the café. The man seated three tables away, who had mostly been hidden behind his newspaper as the two men had sat absorbed in conversation, watched them pause at the cash desk and then depart.

'That's odd,' Clem Hargraves murmured to himself. 'That was Chief Inspector Calthorp — no doubt of it. Now I just wonder if he is going to start pestering Elsa again?'

He considered a list he had pulled from his pocket, places whereat he was forced to call before they closed. It did not leave any time for a detour to Midhampton.

'See her this evening,' he decided. 'If that isn't too late I may be able to put her on her guard.'

* * *

After profuse thanks and insisting on paying up to date, Castle and his wife and daughter departed from Tudor Cottage about five-thirty and Elsa was once again left to herself. Though she would not admit it, even to herself, the place seemed unbearably dull after the trio's departure. She thought of doing some writing and then shook her head irritably. She was not in the mood. Finally she threw herself into an armchair and sat brooding, until a strident ringing at the front door startled her. Surprised, and glad of the change, she hurried through the hall.

Clem Hargraves was in the porch, his homely face looking unusually serious.

'Oh, then you're still here!' he exclaimed. 'I was getting worried about you.'

'Yes — still here,' Elsa acknowledged.

'Car's out front,' Clem said. 'Feel like coming for a run? It's a nice evening.'

'All right,' Elsa assented. 'I'll be with you in a few moments.'

He relaxed against the front doorway and waited whilst the girl sped upstairs. She reflected as she made her outdoor preparations that Clem Hargraves could not have come at a better time to relieve the monotony. Before long she had joined him in the porch and they went down the pathway together to his car.

'You're looking unusually bothered, Clem,' she told him at length, as he drove slowly down the sunny lane. 'What's the trouble?'

'I came really to warn you,' he

explained. 'You haven't seen that Scotland Yard inspector again, I suppose?'

'Not since the other evening when you saw him.'

'Well I think you will be doing, and before long. He was in the Guildford district this afternoon. I had to be there too on business and I dropped in at a café. I'd just got seated when I noticed Calthorp a few tables away. I promptly put up my newspaper, not having any desire to be mixed up with the gent. He gave me a grilling the other day, you know.'

'He did? And this is the first chance you've had to tell me about it?'

'Afraid so; been extremely busy. Besides, I've not been at all sure just how you'd receive me. Since you turned down my proposal so flatly I can't see really why we go on as we do. Not much point in it, is there?' he asked moodily.

'I've been thinking things over a bit since then,' Elsa replied quietly. 'At that time my nerves were pretty well in rags — what with Clive vanishing so mysteriously, and then the police coming after me. It was hardly the time to think about getting engaged. Now, though — '

Clem brightened. 'You mean there's still a chance, after all? Gosh, Elsa, if only you would! You know I've never thought of anybody else but you in spite of the differences of opinion we've had. I still say that I could protect you against all comers if we were married.'

'The trouble is,' Elsa sighed, 'that I can't feel free until I know what the law has decided concerning Clive. I couldn't marry with the thought hanging over me that one day the police might find enough evidence to arrest me. It wouldn't be fair to you — to either of us.'

'I'd risk that, if you would. You're alone too much, Elsa! There's no earthly reason why you should wage this fight all by yourself . . . Anyway, maybe you'll soon know something one way or the other now Calthorp is in the vicinity.'

'When he interviewed you, how much did he ask?' Elsa inquired, thinking.

'Matter of fact he almost proved to his own satisfaction that I might have killed Clive Hexley, for reasons of jealousy.

Then he asked me for a full statement of all my movements from the day Hexley had been seen in this district. I sent it to the Yard and have heard nothing since. Damned silly, I call it! As if I'd *kill* Hexley! I didn't like the way he snatched you, of course, but I'm no killer.'

'Did he ask you anything concerning me?'

'Oh, one or two things.' Clem gave a shrug. 'Just wanted to know the extent of your association with me, and so forth. I told him and he seemed satisfied. Anyway, you can see why I didn't want to get involved with him again in the café. He's got a nasty habit of making you admit things whether you want to or not.'

'You're sure he didn't see you?'

'Couldn't have done or he'd surely have come over and said something. No, I'm sure he didn't see me. He was too deep in conversation with a white-haired old buffer for that. Some pal of his, I suppose.'

Elsa was silent for a moment or two as the car moved on slowly through the countryside, aiming at nowhere in particular. Then she gave a little start.

'White-haired old buffer?' she repeated. 'Do you mean silver-haired?'

'Same thing, isn't it? What about it?'

'Just a moment — what did he look like, this man Calthorp was talking to?' There was a glint in Elsa's gray eyes. 'Was he big and fat, with about three chins and a round face?'

'Yes — he was.' Clem glanced in surprise. 'What's the matter? Who cares, anyway?'

'I do!' Elsa snapped. 'Stop the car a moment. I've something I want to sort out.'

Clem obeyed and then sat looking at the girl questioningly. The bitterness that had come into her expression startled him.

'That man,' she said slowly, her mouth taut, 'has been in my home with his wife and daughter since yesterday tea-time. They only left about half an hour before you turned up this evening.'

'What on earth were they doing staying with you?' Clem asked blankly.

Elsa gave him the facts and he whistled softly.

'Whew! Sure it's the same chap?'

'It must have been! The description fits exactly, and I know he was out at the time, supposedly hiring a car in which to take home his wife and daughter. The fact that you saw him talking so earnestly to Calthorp settles it for me. He was a spy! Spying on me! And I thought he was a perfectly genuine lawyer . . . Of all the rotten, low down tricks!'

'The police,' Clem said grimly, 'will attempt anything — but it can't do them much good unless they get something out of it, and I imagine you were smart enough to make sure that this chap Bennington — or whatever his real name is — didn't find out anything. In any case, you've nothing to hide, have you?'

'That's not the point! How dare he come probing and peeping into my home in that underhand fashion? I'll go to Scotland Yard and demand an explanation! Yes, that's what I'll do!'

'Now wait a minute,' Clem said, gripping her arm. 'Don't go off half cocked, Elsa: think the thing out first. Just how much good do you suppose this detective did himself by being in your home? There couldn't be anything worth his attention, could there?'

'Well . . . ' Elsa frowned worriedly. 'Not as far as I know. You see, it depends what he was looking for. The police get up to such tricks when they want information. That man may have found something which, used in the right way, could perhaps form evidence to prove that I killed Clive, or something — and I'd perhaps have an awful job to talk myself out of it. As far as I know there was nothing he could have found, but just the same . . . '

'Don't you worry, he didn't find anything,' Clem assured her. 'It was a dirty plant, I agree with you — but it didn't prove of any use. As for your dashing to the Yard to make a complaint I should go easy. If you do that, and make a row, it will make it look as though you may be guilty and afraid that something has been discovered. If you take my advice you'll do nothing.'

'Yes . . . Perhaps you're right.' Elsa sat reflecting. 'Just the same,' she added, 'I think there may be something I can do to find out how much that white-haired old liar *did* discover.'

'And that is?'

'Never mind. Just leave me to handle things in my own way, Clem. Drive me back home, will you? I want a chance to think this one out. I'll show *him* whether he'll creep into my home like that!'

14

Towards ten o'clock the same evening Chief Inspector Calthorp called on Dr. Castle at his Hampstead home and was shown into the lounge where the big psychiatrist, his wife, and Brenda were seated at their ease. Calthorp half motioned with his hand as Castle attempted to rise.

'Don't trouble, doc,' he said. 'Heaving all that around isn't too easy for you, I know . . . Glad to see you back in your native haunt. Good evening, Mrs. Castle — '

'And Brenda,' Castle murmured, wheezing, 'whom you have not met before. Brendy, this is Chief Inspector Calthorp of Scotland Yard.'

Brenda bobbed up, shook hands rather shyly, and then sat down again with her eyes rather wide.

'You actually don't wear your hat inside the house, inspector,' she exclaimed. 'I thought all policemen did that.'

'My daughter,' Castle explained sadly, 'extracts her education from the movies. Heaven knows why I pay college fees . . . Anyway, Calthorp, sit down. Have a drink?'

'No, thanks all the same. Bit too late. I'm on my way home but I thought I'd drop in and tell you about — er — Well, you know. The hanky.'

'No need to keep it a secret,' Castle said, smiling. 'My wife and Brendy know all the facts. Since we got back home I've given them the details up to date: they're entitled to it since they've helped me so well. All right, what about the hanky?'

'The blood group is A-B.'

'Ah!' Castle's blue eyes gleamed. 'Then I think that ties up most satisfactorily with the blood on the belt and handbag. It is Miss Farraday's.'

'In that I agree with you — but it does also bring us to a dead stop without us knowing Hexley's group. I've been racking my brains to try and think where we might find some clue about that — without result. I've been through his

262

studio, as I told you, seen the doctor who fixed him up. Done everything, I imagine.'

'And you have been to his flat?' Castle asked, musing.

'Yes; mainly to try and find some clues and also to get those hair combings. I found nothing there that would help us with the blood-group.'

'It's a confoundedly awkward problem,' Castle muttered. 'Best thing I can do is have a look round for myself. I'm not doubting your thoroughness, Calthorp, but we work in different ways. Tomorrow we'll take a look at that studio and his flat. If we get nothing out of those we'll have to think further.'

'Okay, doc; it's up to you. At the same time maybe you can figure out how that hair on the handbag comes to be Hexley's. It has me pretty well stumped, unless we accept the rather dubious conclusion that Miss Farraday had one or two of his hairs on her own clothes and used them. But I don't see how she could know they were his. One picks up all manner of stray hairs, especially after a train journey.'

'That,' Castle said, aiming a reproving glance, 'is a distinctly poor theory for you, Calthorp. I'm convinced you need a drink.'

In spite of Calthorp's protests he heaved to his feet and went over to the sideboard . . . and whilst he was doing it Elsa Farraday was seated in a night train for London.

Alone in the corner of her compartment her lips were tight and her eyes filled with cold bitterness. The 'invasion' of Bennington was, to her, both puzzling and alarming. Thinking back, she could not remember that she had said anything particularly incriminating, but knowing the ways of the police she was not *sure*. Somewhere she might have made an unwitting admission of some kind. The exact reason for planting a detective in her home — for as yet she had no idea of Castle's real profession — was something which baffled her.

So far in her efforts to discover 'Mr. Bennington's' real occupation and address she had drawn a blank. First she had tried the garage where the wrecked car had been taken, but the proprietor had told her that 'Bennington' had traded in the car as scrap, it being damaged beyond repair and taken a nominal price for it. Her inquiries after that, which had taken her to Guildford, had been confined to calling upon all possible garages and asking for particulars about a silver-haired man who had hired a private car. She had at last tracked down the garage, and only learned that his name was 'Bennington' and his address the Middle Temple London. Since she knew that much already it had not advanced her any.

But at least the Middle Temple seemed a likely starting point to reopen her investigation — hence her present journey to London, her reservation made in advance with the hotel at which she usually stopped when in the city.

Once she arrived in town she had her taxi driver detour to the Middle Temple on the way to the hotel, despite his protests that it was useless going in that direction at that hour of night. Outside

Vance Chambers in the famous old legal quarter of the metropolis the taxi pulled up and Elsa stepped out.

In the glimmer of the street lamps she peered at the brass plates outside Vance Chambers, but nowhere was there a sign of Adam Bennington, Barrister-at-Law. There was Todmore, Cranstall, and Bury — but no Bennington.

'Told you it was no use, miss,' the taxi driver said, watching her. 'These law offices shut around five o'clock of an evening — '

'I know that,' Elsa told him curtly. 'I'm simply checking up on a name — or trying to. Bennington, a barrister. His address should be here, but apparently it isn't.'

'Sorry, lady . . . Strite to your hotel now?'

'Yes, I suppose so,' Elsa sighed; then she hesitated before climbing back into the taxi. 'Look, do you often drive through this quarter?'

'More times 'n I can count. Bin doin' it for forty year nearly — takin' these legal blokes to an' from the station chiefly. Why?'

'You've never heard of one of then called Bennington, I suppose?'

'Sorry, miss. Don't know their names anyway — Or only a few of 'em. Bennington? What's he look like? Sort o' bloke you might know if you saw 'im again?'

'I imagine so. About six feet, very stout, and silver-haired. Be about fifty-five or sixty years of age.'

'Oh, *'im*!' the taxi driver ejaculated. 'Why, of course I know 'im! Drive 'im many a time from the station to 'ere, and from 'ere to his place in 'Arley Street. You're miles off your track, miss. He isn't a lawyer, an' 'is name isn't Bennington neither.'

'Harley Street?' Elsa repeated sharply. 'That's the doctor's section, isn't it?'

'Course it is, miss — an' that's what 'e is. Castle's 'is name. Dr. Adam Castle. 'E's one them blokes who fiddle with your nerves an' brain. A — er — psycho . . . Whatever you call it.'

'Psychologist?' Elsa suggested, in a low voice.

'Aye, that's it. I'll swear that's the bloke

you want, lady. Big, genial feller with — '

'Drive me to my hotel!' Elsa interrupted, and stepping inside the taxi she slammed the door and relaxed in the upholstery. She clenched her fists and muttered to herself.

'So that's it! Not a detective but a psychiatrist! He was planted there to study me. Not to look for clues. To probe into my mind, to find out why things are as they are . . . I never even thought of such a thing! But there's an answer to it. Once I'm sure it is the same man. He has a daughter, a girl who's never known a moment's unhappiness, to judge from the look of her — Analyze *me*, will he?'

* * *

At ten o'clock the following morning, Castle and Chief Inspector Calthorp arrived at Hexley's closed studio in Chelsea. Calthorp obtained the key from the janitor and opened the place up. Pensively Castle waddled in, hands in trousers pockets and small black hat on the back of his silvery head.

'Obviously a Bohemian!' he commented. 'Of all the confoundedly untidy places!'

Calthorp grinned an acknowledgment and led the way into the adjoining dressing room, remarking:

'If there's anything at all we're likely to find, doc, it'll be in here. I've searched already, but see what you can do.'

Castle lumbered after him and, breathing hard, stooped low down to shelves and reached high up to cupboards, ransacking both. The additional litter amidst that already accumulated did not seem to matter. Certainly Castle was thorough, more so than Calthorp had been. He examined crockery, a face flannel, and particularly an old razor blade that he finally tossed away.

'Nothing on that,' he sighed. 'Dammit, the man couldn't even cut his whiskers like a gentleman and leave us a blood trace.'

'Just the same, that may be an angle,' Calthorp said thoughtfully. 'And one I hadn't thought of. What about the old razor blades at his flat? There might be some. They are always pretty difficult things to get rid of.'

Castle nodded. 'Yes, it's worth a try. You hop over there, Calthorp, and see what you can find. You've already been through this place, anyway. I'll see if I can find anything here.'

The chief inspector hurried away and Castle continued his prowl alone, gazing thoughtfully about him at intervals. He gave two smocks particular attention, examining the paint splashes on them, and finally he shook his head. Apparently, from the absence of blood traces, Hexley had not been wearing a smock when he had met with the accident with the dagger.

Beaten so far Castle wandered into the studio and began an almost interminable exploration of everything within sight. Dusters in particular he studied minutely, and the handles of the paint brushes. The half-completed paintings also claimed his attention, but he arrived no nearer a solution to his problem. Finally he sat down, took off his hat and felt for his pipe. When Calthorp arrived back some thirty minutes later he found the psychiatrist smoking solemnly and gazing in front of him.

'Well, any luck?' the chief inspector asked.

'The same question applies to you.' Castle slanted a blue eye. 'What did you find at Hexley's flat?'

'Nothing . . . Or rather, almost nothing. We might do better if we pull down the building in which Hexley's flat is situated.'

'What!'

'Sounds queer, I know,' Calthorp admitted moodily, 'but it's a fact.' He sat down and lighted a cigarette, fanning himself with his hat as the sun blazed through the opaque glass roof. He continued: 'In the bathroom of his flat I couldn't find any old razor blades at first, then after looking around I caught sight of one in a small crack in the plaster-cast wall. I tried to grab it, but I was too hasty and knocked it out of reach. I borrowed thin-jawed pliers and a torch from the proprietor, but the blade had gone. It must have dropped down between the space of the party walls separating Hexley's flat from the one next to it. And since the walls go down seven floors I assume that the blade is behind the basement party wall — and maybe there are dozens of others like it.'

'In other words,' Castle grinned, 'Hexley solved man's greatest problem — what to do with old razor blades. So he put them through a crack in the wall, did he? Mmmm. All right, in spite of inconvenience and compensation to pay, the party wall in the basement must be broken through and the base of the gap between the walls examined for old blades. On one of them there might be traces of blood from a facial cut. It's our last chance, Calthorp.'

'Yes, I think you're right,' the chief inspector admitted. 'And I hope the A.C. is reasonable when I tell him what we have to do.'

The psychiatrist did not comment further. He was smoking absently and staring hard at the wooden floor of the studio. Then suddenly he took his pipe from his mouth and got to his feet.

Without speaking he began a tour of the studio, examining in his travels each and every one of the paintings he could find, both on the floor and on the easels.

'That's interesting,' he said at length, pondering.

'What is? What's wrong?'

'In none of these paintings is there anything of a chocolate-brown shade — not even in this one of Elsa Farraday, half completed. Reds, browns, and russets, but no chocolate-brown . . . Let me see now.'

Castle picked up the palette and inspected it, then he studied each tube of paint. Turning, he said:

'Still no chocolate brown, or combination of shades to make that color.'

'What about it?' Calthorp asked in wonder.

'Look!' And Dr. Castle pointed.

Calthorp gazed at the wooden floor near the easel containing Elsa Farraday's portrait. The floor was liberally spattered with paint spots, a condition which Elsa herself had noticed when she had first entered the studio — but under the easel there were at least six comparatively new chocolate brown stains, varying in size.

'Good heavens, do you think — ?' Calthorp leapt up suddenly.

'There's no paint to account for those stains: it could be blood from Hexley's injured hand,' Castle said. 'The best thing you can do is get a man over here quickly to make a test with bendizine and hydrogen peroxide.'

Calthorp did not hesitate for a moment. He hurried from the studio and downstairs to the nearest telephone. Then he came back and with Castle contemplated the marks pensively.

'Just about how bloodstains would look after all this time,' he commented. 'Maybe I shan't have to pull down that party wall after all. I surely hope not.'

'On the other hand you may,' Castle told him. 'If this stuff on the floor *is* blood it does not say that it is Hexley's. It might belong to anybody who has been in the studio, or even to an animal. Bendizine is no respecter of species, unfortunately. However, let us not consider such a coincidence at the moment. The point is this: If we can find anything on the razor blades that we know Hexley had used to shave himself, and it should match this stuff — if blood it is — then we have *proof.*'

'Right enough,' Calthorp agreed, a gleam in his eye.

With some difficulty he kept his patience until at last the man from the forensic department with his little 'bag of tricks' arrived. He nodded as the chief inspector indicated the spots and immediately went down on his knees to commence work. Carefully he scraped up the deposit from one of the spots and placed it on a strip of filter-paper glued to a glass slide. Then he added the drop of combined bendizine and hydrogen peroxide.

Instantly the chocolate-brown spot turned a bluish green and spread quickly over the filter paper.

'Blood!' Calthorp exclaimed in delight. 'You guessed right, doc! Okay,' he added to the forensic expert, 'take up the rest of this stain deposit and have it analyzed for blood-grouping right away. Send the report to my office.'

'Right, sir.'

Calthorp waited until the job was completed and the man had gone, then he turned again to the psychiatrist.

'That settles that. I suppose we'd better see now what we can do about that party wall business.'

'No doubt of it — and there's certainly no need to ask the A.C. whether you should or not. Dammit, man, it only needs the removal of a brick from the basement wall, roughly on a line with the bathroom seven floors higher up. The rest is simply a matter of a small magnet on the end of a stick. Come — I'll show you.'

Content to leave developments to the unorthodox Castle, Calthorp locked up the studio and then followed the psychiatrist downstairs and out to the waiting police car. On the way to Hexley's flat Castle made two unavailing attempts to buy a magnet; but the third time at a radio and electrical shop he was successful and emerged beaming, with a horseshoe magnet clasped in his podgy hand.

'The yard owes me for this, apart from my usual fee,' he said dryly, handing over the paid bill. 'I don't suppose we need to buy a hammer and chisel. The proprietor should have those.'

The proprietor had, but for all that he did not appear particularly attracted to the idea of having the basement wall hammered through.

'In other words, my dear sir, you would prefer that we get the necessary authority to *make* you give permission?' Castle inquired, his enormous frame towering over the small vinegar-faced man.

'I doubt if you could ever get permission to do a thing like this,' the man snapped. 'The law has certain advantages, I know, but when it comes to smashing up the property of a law-abiding tax payer I — '

'Upon your co-operation, either forced or voluntary, there may depend a life.' Castle told him solemnly. 'To get the authority will mean delay. In that time an innocent person might be grievously wronged. You knew Mr. Hexley and he was a good tenant. Do you think it is altogether public-spirited of you to take this attitude when taking a brick out of the wall might produce his murderer?'

'Murderer? Behind *there*?'

'I stand corrected,' Castle murmured. 'I should have said the necessary clue to perhaps indict his murderer. The clue being old razor blades.'

The proprietor sighed. 'Oh, all right. The inspector mentioned about the razor blade business. I can see I'll get no peace if I don't agree. Come on down to the basement and I'll give you an idea where the straight line from Hexley's bathroom should finish.'

After taking a hammer and chisel from the tool chest he led the way out of his office, along a corridor, and down a flight of stone steps which opened on to a wide underground area with plain brick walls. Electric bulbs gleamed at intervals from a steel conduit

Castle and Calthorp stood watching as the proprietor stood in various positions, his head on one side as he assessed the

278

right-hand wall. Finally he nodded and tapped a certain spot.

'Be about here,' he said.

'Thanks.' Castle moved over and took the hammer and chisel from him. 'Now let's see what we can do. Here, Calthorp — you are slimmer than I. Get busy.'

Calthorp went down on his knees and began operations, the proprietor watching and wincing at intervals. Nor did the bland expression on Castle's round face make him seem any the happier.

In ten minutes Calthorp had smashed through the mortar and eased the brick out gently. At Castle's request the proprietor searched round for and presently found a long stick. With the magnet secured to the end of it Calthorp eased it into the hole in the wall and fished about carefully. When he finally withdrew the magnet all manner of metallic objects were clinging to it. There were razor blades by the dozen, old and rusted; ancient tin tacks, pins, metallic bits from piping shavings . . .

Carefully Castle picked off the razor blades, nearly three dozen of them, and tipped them into an envelope. The remaining rubbish he threw back into the cavity and Calthorp replaced the brick.

'Well, not as bad as I'd expected,' the proprietor admitted, a trifle mollified. 'Get what you wanted, gents?'

'Definitely,' Castle responded. 'Now, if you can find us some mortar we can put — '

'Never mind that. I'll patch the brick up for myself.'

'Splendid! Then we'd better be on our way, Calthorp.'

The chief inspector nodded and in fifteen minutes he and the psychiatrist were back at Scotland Yard, in the forensic department. In silence they watched the experts get to work on the blades, whilst another group were conducting a precipitin test on the deposit that had been removed from the studio floor.

Amongst the razor blades only two in the three dozen had worthwhile stains upon them, turning blue under the bendizine and hydrogen peroxide test. Castle glanced at Calthorp and noted the look of profound satisfaction.

'Hurry it up,' the chief inspector said. 'We'll wait.' To hurry a precipitin test, however, was something chemically impossible, and accordingly it was towards noon when a fuming Calthorp and imperturbable Castle received — in the chief inspector's office — the information for which they were waiting.

'Both groups are O, sir,' the expert said, putting the classification card on the table.

'They are, eh?' Calthorp gave a grim smile. 'All right — many thanks.'

He picked up the cards as the expert went out and Castle gave his slow, fleshy chuckle.

'Well, Calthorp, there it is. Hexley's group is O — quite a common group — and that on the handbag, belt, and handkerchief was A-B, the *rare* group. In other words, Miss Farraday fixed things up for herself. The best thing we can do now is to confront her with this information and see how she reacts. I have the feeling that she'll break down.'

15

About the time the chief inspector and Castle were awaiting results Elsa Farraday was studying the telephone directory in her hotel. Finally she ran her finger along an entry —

Castle, Adam. Neurologist and Psychiatrist. M Mordaunt Chambers, Harley Street. Central 1695 (Residence: The Elms, Heston Grove, Hampstead. HAMpstead 78)

'Hampstead,' she mused, making a note; then she put the directory aside and walked over to one of the telephone booths, closing the door tightly. She dialled Central 1695 and waited. After a moment or two a woman's pleasant voice spoke.

'Dr. Castle's chambers. Who is speaking, please?'

Elsa took full stock of the inflexions in the woman's voice and responded in a voice utterly unlike her own — hesitating and nervous.

'Oh — er — I'm Miss — Miss Prentiss. Could I see — see the doctor this morning, do you think? It's most ur — urgent.'

'I'm so sorry, Miss Prentiss. Dr. Castle is out on business for the day. He has cancelled all appointments. Tomorrow perhaps?'

'Tomorrow? Oh . . . Er — who is that speak — speaking?'

'I am the doctor's secretary. Shall I make an appointment for you for tomorrow?'

'Ye-yes, maybe that would be as well, Miss — er — '

'Taytham.'

'Yes, Miss Taytham. To — tomorrow, then. About what time?'

'Would eleven o'clock suit you?'

'That will suit me fi — fine thanks. I'll be there. And — and I'll ask for you. That will give me con — confidence.'

'Good!' the secretary laughed. 'Tomorrow then, Miss Prentiss.'

Elsa rang off, waited for a moment or

two, and then dialed the number of Castle's home. The voice of the maid, answered her. Putting two of her fingers over the mouthpiece to distort the sound Elsa said:

'Mrs. Castle, please. This is Miss Taytham speaking.'

'Oh yes, Miss Taytham. Just a moment.'

Elsa waited, making up her mind what she was going to say, then as Mrs. Castle's familiar voice came over the wire Elsa said experimentally:

'Hello, Mrs. Castle — '

'Good morning, Miss Taytham.' Elsa breathed in relief as she realized there was evidently no other designation for the secretary. 'Is there anything wrong?'

'No, nothing wrong, Mrs. Castle. I have a message here that the doctor has left. I've only just come in; been out on a special call. It says — 'Telephone home and have my daughter come here by eleven o'clock if possible.''

'Brenda?' Mrs. Castle sounded surprised. 'You've no idea why, I suppose?'

'Not officially, but I think it has something to do with that Clive Hexley business which the doctor is working on. I have the details, of course — confidentially.'

'Oh well, then, in that case I'll see she comes right away. She has only just got time. Fortunately she's at home. Thanks, Miss Taytham; I'll see to it.'

'Right. Goodbye, Mrs. Castle.'

Elsa put down the telephone and hurried out of the booth. The elevator took her to the floor on which her room was situated and five minutes later she was in a taxi speeding towards Harley Street. Her calculations, that she would be there before Brenda could arrive from Hampstead, were correct. It was ten minutes after she had arrived within a few yards of Mordaunt Chambers before the youthful figure of Brenda tumbled from a taxi and paid the driver.

Elsa moved forward silently, her hand closing round the small automatic in her loose topcoat. Just as Brenda was about to go up the steps to Mordaunt Chambers Elsa arranged the 'collision.'

'Oh, I'm so sorry — ' Brenda began, then she gave a start of amazement. 'Why, it's Elsa Farraday! Of all people! I *am* glad to see you again.'

'Are you?' Elsa asked coldly. 'It isn't mutual, Brenda. I have not much regard for daughters who help their fathers to spy!'

Brenda was far too inexperienced to tackle this statement offhand. She just stared, gradually realizing that her father's activities were no longer a secret.

'Then — you know?' she asked uneasily.

'I do. And you needn't waste your time going in here, either. It was not Miss Taytham who 'phoned your mother; it was I . . . I think you and I should have a little chat, Brenda.'

'But — But I — '

'Now!' Elsa added flatly, and, for a moment withdrew her hand to disclose the automatic. 'I'm not going to pull my punches, Brenda,' she added. 'Do as I tell you or it will be the worse for you.'

Brenda descended the steps again and Elsa took hold of her arm firmly, leading her up the street until they reached a taxi stand.

'Get in,' Elsa ordered, motioning to the vehicle, and, to the driver she gave the name of her hotel.

'What are you going to do?' Brenda asked anxiously, fear plainly visible in her wide blue eyes.

'I want you to come with me to Midhampton,' Elsa responded. 'To my home. I've got something there that I think you should know about. In fact it is hardly a case of my wanting you to: you have no choice. We are going to my hotel, where I intend to collect my things and pay my bill — and if you know what's good for you you'll stay right beside me.'

'But you can't mean you'd shoot me if I don't? In a crowded hotel?'

'I would if necessary and take the consequences,' Elsa replied coldly. 'If you don't believe it, just disobey orders.'

Brenda slowly relaxed, staring worriedly in front of her. Not knowing what kind of a mood Elsa was in she was afraid to take a chance — and Elsa knew it. Where an adult would have called her bluff, and probably overpowered her, this sixteen-year-old was in a complete daze, and because of it she did as she was told, never making a single wrong move when the hotel was reached and she went into the lounge ahead of Elsa.

Fifteen minutes later they were in a train bound for Guildford with connections to Midhampton — and it was only as the train drew out of London with steady speed that it dawned on Brenda Castle that she had been abducted.

★　★　★

It was early afternoon when, after a lunch in Guildford — an exceedingly strained affair — Elsa escorted Brenda up the front path of Tudor Cottage. Twice during the mile walk from the village Brenda had thought of making a dash for it, and then had changed her mind. Here, in the deserted countryside, there would be nothing to stop Elsa doing just as she pleased, and in her plainly vindictive mood Brenda had little doubt that she would perhaps shoot, perhaps even to kill.

'What is this something you want me to know about?' she demanded in sudden desperation, as Elsa put down her suitcase in the porch and took a key from her pocket. 'Do you realize what you're doing, Miss Farraday? This is kidnapping, and there's a big penalty for that!'

Elsa only gave her a contemptuous glance, opened the front door, and motioned her into the hall. She put down her suitcase just inside the doorway, snapped the catch on the front door as she closed it, and then nodded toward the lounge.

Brenda went in alone, gazing anxiously around her upon the quietness and the soft rays of the summer afternoon sunlight.

'So you're anxious to know why you're here, are you?' Elsa asked, throwing off her hat and taking the automatic from her pocket but retaining it in her hand. 'Well I'll tell you . . . I'm going to kill you!'

Brenda sat down heavily, staring up at her. The statement did not seem to so much shock her as amaze her. She looked as though she just could not credit it.

'But why?' she asked. 'What have I done? Just because I helped my father?'

'That's one reason, but there's a better one. I don't like you, Brenda — and I never have, from the moment I first met you. You are carefree, irresponsible; you've never known what it is to suffer anything. You, who cannot know the first thing about a person like me, dared to come into my home to find out what you could about me! You, who hardly know yet what life is about! If you think I'm going to let you get away with that you're vastly mistaken.'

'What you really mean is that you're jealous!' Brenda declared boldly. 'Yes, that's it! You've had a rotten life up to now and you don't see why I should have a good one. That's it, isn't it?'

'If you like to look at it that way,' Elsa assented. 'However, I do not see why your father, after the trick he played on me, poking and prying and doing his best to discover all he could concerning me, should have the pleasure of your society any longer. Nor do I see why you, who don't know what unhappiness is, should go on living in such blissful ignorance to perhaps help your father in further underhand schemes. With your disappearance, Brenda, your father will come straight here. It won't take him long to guess who it was who spoke to your mother on the 'phone. When he comes I'll deal with him as I intend to deal with you. He'll walk straight into the trap and I'll be ready for him.'

Brenda said nothing. She still sat and stared, half wondering, half horrified.

'I could have shot you at any time on the journey here,' Elsa continued, 'only it would simply have meant that I'd have been immediately arrested and your father would have escaped. As things are going to be he'll be one of the first people here, looking for you. And your body,' Elsa finished, 'will not vanish in a swamp as Clive Hexley's did. You see, without the body being found I can't be charged with murder. Nor, for that matter, does it seem I can even be arrested. I had expected that I would have been. All the country would have talked about me; and then,' Elsa added slowly, half smiling to herself, 'I would have been released because of no corpus delicti. Think how

291

much attention I would have got, how I would have beaten the law at its own game! But I was cheated out of it. Inspector Calthorp did not arrest me after all.'

'No,' Brenda whispered, 'I know he didn't. Dad told me about that.'

'This time the body — your body — will be found. And, if my plan is right, so will your father's. I'll be arrested for murder, of course, but I don't mind. There is no death sentence any more, remember. I shall spend fifteen years in jail, I expect, but since I have nothing left to live for anyway that doesn't worry me in the least. Interest in living vanished for me when Clive Hexley died.'

'You didn't love him!' Brenda declared. 'My father told me as much, and he told my mother so as well. You couldn't have done because you broke off your engagement to him when he cut his hand with that dagger — '

'Yes — because he could not give me the fame in a portrait which I had expected. But other things happened after that, Brenda — things your father has never known about, or that Scotland Yard inspector either. You see, Clive Hexley really loved me and, deep down, I loved him — in spite of the thing that had happened to his hand. He followed me here to this house. He talked, he pleaded, he explained. Then it was that I realized how much I really meant to him. He even said that, difficult though it might be at first, he would learn to paint with his left hand. He cared that much for me. He could still give me that fame, that reflected glory, for which I longed — and still long. Now I can only gain it by making Calthorp arrest me for a genuine murder. My notoriety will be that of being a jail-bird perhaps, but it will be better than nothing at all.'

'You're crazy!' Brenda breathed. 'My father said you were — and he was right.'

'Because I try and seize on the opportunities and joys which a thrashed and beaten childhood never gave me?' Elsa demanded venomously. 'Yes, if that's craziness, I *am* crazy! But I was telling you,' she resumed, speaking as though the memory haunted her. 'Clive Hexley came

293

back here and we patched up our differences. It was agreed that I should return to London and that he would get the best surgeon possible to see what could be done about his hand. I was to return on the Saturday, the day after he came here. I would then become re-engaged to him. He was going to give me my engagement ring back but I wouldn't take it: I thought it was unlucky and asked for a new one. Then he left here . . .'

Elsa was silent for a long time, reflecting. Brenda did not dare to utter a word. Fascinated, she waited for the next.

'I can see it now,' Elsa mused, pressing finger and thumb to her eyes for a moment. 'I can recall every horrible incident. He was late for his train and decided to take the short cut across Barraclough's Swamp. I explained to him as he stood facing me at the back gate of the garden that the left path was the safe one and the right one the false — But don't you see,' she breathed, 'he had his *back* to the swamp when I gave him those directions, so that when he turned round left became right and right became left. It was too late to stop him. He ran because he was in a hurry, and sank into the mire!

'I dashed after him and did all in my power to save him — but I could only just reach him from the safe part where I was standing. It was no use. I shouted for help; I screamed for it — but out here nobody heard me. He went down. I was left with nothing but the few hairs that had caught under my nails when I'd made my last desperate effort to save him . . . I don't know how long it was before I came back here — stunned, unable to think. I kept looking at those hairs, which had caught in my nails. I realized that everything had gone — Clive, my chances of fame, my future, his life . . . '

'And so, Miss Farraday, in your insane search for reflected glory you hit on the idea of making it seem as if you had killed Mr. Hexley and thrown him in the swamp?'

Elsa twirled round violently and stared at the doorway. The vast, looming figure of Castle was standing there, and behind him the figure of Chief Inspector Calthorp.

'How did you get here?' Elsa shrieked, whirling up her automatic.

'It is really quite simple.' Castle advanced slowly, staring at the girl and ignoring the automatic. 'The inspector and I found the last positive links this morning to prove that you did not kill Clive Hexley as you said — and we decided to come here and inform you that you had ceased to be of interest to the police in *that* respect — but we were going to find out the real circumstances concerning his disappearance. Now that no longer signifies, either. Since you have told everything to my daughter, in the belief that she would never have the chance to repeat it . . .'

'If you come any closer I'll shoot you!' Elsa snapped.

'No you won't,' Castle told her. 'You are not a murderess at heart, Miss Farraday; there's far too much buried generosity in your nature for that. You're simply embittered and profoundly unhappy because of it. Marry a man who has your interests at heart and who will take good care of you. You do not *really* want fame by becoming a murderess. You know you don't. You only think of achieving it that way because there seems to be no other.'

'Why can't you leave me alone, Dr. Castle — ?'

'Put that gun down, Miss Farraday,' Castle ordered, his voice quiet, as he paused a yard away from her. 'Go on — put it down.'

Elsa hesitated for quite half a minute, then at the steady compulsion in the psychiatrist's blue eyes she complied. She threw the gun on to the table where it rattled noisily. Sinking into a chair she ran her hands through her thick dark hair.

'You still haven't explained how you come to be here,' she muttered.

'I rang up my wife just before setting off from London to tell her that I would not be home for lunch — my usual procedure,' Castle responded. 'She told me my secretary had telephoned concerning Brenda. I checked back on my secretary, and guessed the remainder. So the inspector and I came on here ahead of you, let ourselves in with a master-key, and waited. I was pretty sure that, convinced you were alone with Brenda, you would probably break down and tell everything. It's a common practice of an egocentric to explain every detail to an intended victim, knowing that the victim cannot — or would not be able — to repeat it. And you ran true to form.'

'How on earth did you get here before us?' Brenda asked in amazement. 'We came straight away by train.'

'We chartered a police 'plane from London to Guildford which gave us an hour's advantage over you,' Castle explained. 'Nor did we stop to have lunch, as you probably did.'

'All right,' Elsa said bitterly, 'so you've definitely proven that I didn't kill Clive — and you overheard the truth as to how he died. That means the police have nothing more to do with me, doesn't it?'

'It does,' the chief inspector told her quietly. 'Your word alone would never have been accepted, of course. It was the checking of the blood-groups which did it. You deliberately used your own blood on that bag.'

'Yes. Because I was sure you couldn't check it without Clive's body. It was simple. I purposely pricked my finger — '

'As I made you prick it again on the rose thorns,' Castle commented, and he smiled blandly at the girl's angry look; then, serious again, he went over to her and put an arm about her shoulders. 'Listen to me, Miss Farraday,' he continued. 'I'm old enough to be your father and in that capacity I'm going to talk to you. You have not, throughout this whole business, performed one really vicious act. Even breaking the engagement was not vicious because you were impelled by something greater than yourself. The reaction of realizing that you would not achieve your object blinded you to everything else. You have admitted that you saw the error of your ways when Hexley followed you here. You lost him in tragic circumstances — that I know. You have tried by various escapisms — such as dressing and behaving as a child, writing thrillers under a pseudonym, and maybe other means which I have not been at pains to find — to break away from the rigors and terrors of your childhood. Don't you understand *one thing*, Miss Farraday? You are *not* a child any longer! The terror of those days has gone, and it will never return. You are free to live as you wish, to be loved, to be taken notice of . . . '

'Will never return,' Elsa repeated, staring at him. Then she said the words over again in something like awe. 'Why, of course! It *can't* return, can it? Somehow I had always thought — '

'That it would? Naturally you have. That has been the mental reaction of the years of terror you endured. Believe me, Miss Farraday, for just one moment — You are perfectly *free*! Childhood has gone, but you can perhaps give to children of your own all the care and happiness which you yourself missed . . . Murder, revenge, those morbid crime thrillers — are not for you. The answer is simple: write by all means, but do away with the horrors and write of life as you find it. It has its sweet side as well as its bitter. And call yourself Elsa Farraday. Then you will achieve that glory you've been looking for — but as yourself, and not as a tragic, furtive, alias.'

'I could, I suppose,' Elsa mused.

'You must,' Castle answered. 'Don't become jealous of the happiness of my daughter here. Be like her. It's within your power. One man is waiting to make you happy — more so than Clive Hexley could perhaps ever have done. I mean Clem Hargraves, of course.'

'If — If I should try this method you suggest, and struggle to outlive the old, would you help me,' Elsa pleaded. 'I feel sure that you could. When you were in my home here I felt safe for the first time in my life; then when I realized *why* you had been here I — '

'Forget that,' Castle suggested, smiling. 'And I will help you with pleasure. But you must come to me at my chambers. That is if, on reflection, you think you need me.'

He said no more. Straightening, he withdrew his hand from Elsa's shoulder and motioned silently to Brenda. She rose and followed him and the chief inspector out of the room.

'I think,' Castle commented, as they went down the front pathway, 'that you can call the case of Hexley definitely finished, Calthorp, just as I am sure that we leave behind us a new Elsa Farraday of whom we may hear more in the future.'

Dr. Castle was right. Three weeks later he, his wife, and Brenda received an invitation from Elsa to be present at her marriage to Clem Hargraves; and at the bottom of the card it said:

You were right, Dr. Castle. Life still does hold a great deal. Elsa Farraday.

THE END

We do hope that you have enjoyed reading this large print book.

Did you know that all of our titles are available for purchase?

We publish a wide range of high quality large print books including:
Romances, Mysteries, Classics
General Fiction
Non Fiction and Westerns

Special interest titles available in large print are:
The Little Oxford Dictionary
Music Book, Song Book
Hymn Book, Service Book

Also available from us courtesy of Oxford University Press:
Young Readers' Dictionary
(large print edition)
Young Readers' Thesaurus
(large print edition)

For further information or a free brochure, please contact us at:
Ulverscroft Large Print Books Ltd.,
The Green, Bradgate Road, Anstey,
Leicester, LE7 7FU, England.
Tel: (00 44) **0116 236 4325**
Fax: (00 44) **0116 234 0205**

Other titles in the
Linford Mystery Library:

THE SISKIYOU TWO-STEP

Richard Hoyt

John Denson, a private investigator, goes to Oregon's North Umpqua River to fish trout but, instead, he finds himself caught up in a net of international intelligence agents and academics. It all starts when the naked body of a girl with a bullet hole between her eyes goes rushing past Denson in the rapids. He embarks on a bizarre search to find the girl's identity and to bring her killer to justice. Strange clues lead to three more corpses, and only the Siskiyou Two-Step saves Denson from being the fourth . . .

THREE MAY KEEP A SECRET

Stella Phillips

The proudest citizens of Dolph Hill would not deny that it was a backwater where nothing ever happened — until, that is, the arrival of handsome, secretive Peter Markland disturbs the surface. After his shocking and violent death, old secrets begin to emerge. Detectives Matthew Furnival and Reg King are put on the case. As they delve through the conflicting mysteries, how will they arrive at the one relevant truth?

SHERLOCK HOLMES: THE WAY OF ALL FLESH

Daniel Ward

Sherlock Holmes is called in to investigate when the body of an Italian diplomat is discovered in the River Thames, his torso horrifically mutilated. Fearing the political repercussions — the diplomat being in London to initiate talks regarding a secret naval treaty between the two nations — the Government entrust Holmes with the delicate task of uncovering the truth behind the brutal murder. Events take a shocking turn, however, when a young solicitor is found slain in the East End, his body similarly mutilated . . .